Tempting Justice
A Tempting Nights Romance
Book Three

MICHELLE WINDSOR

Michelle Windsor asserts the right to be identified as the author of this work.

All rights reserved. No part of this book may be reproduced, scanned, distributed, or sold in any printed or electronic form without direct, written permission from the author. Please do not participate in piracy of copyrighted materials in violation of the author's rights.

This is a work of fiction. All names, characters, places, and incidents are products of the author's imagination and are used fictitiously, and any resemblance to actual persons, living or dead, businesses, companies, events, or locales is entirely coincidental.

First published April 2019
Copyright © Michelle Windsor 2019
Published by
Windsor House Publishing
Cover design by Amanda Walker Design Services
Editing provided by Debbie Dumke

**This book contains elements of physical violence.
If this is a trigger for you, please use caution when reading.**

To all the men and women who protect and serve,
this book is for you.
Thank you.

CHAPTER One

~Gabrielle~

My eyes drag open slowly, my vision focusing on the green stack of bills lying on the nightstand in front of me. I roll onto my back, throw an arm across my face, and let out a tired sigh. Just once, I want to wake up to find someone lying next to me, instead of Benjamin Franklin and all his friends. But, I suppose this is part of the job. I provide a service to my clients. They aren't obligated to me once they get what they want. And to appease their guilt, they leave me money, or jewels, and sometimes, even a promise of more.

This is the life of an escort. Well, maybe not all escorts. Technically, my job at Temptations Escort Agency is to accompany a client to whatever function they've requested. Whether it be dinner, a ball, a fundraiser, their plus-one at a wedding reception; you get the idea. My job is to look pretty on their arm and be the best possible date one could imagine, or at least, that they can hire. Everything else; the kissing, the blow-jobs, the hard sex against a closed door, or my wrists bound to bedposts, that's strictly forbidden by the agency. Those arrangements happen between me and the client and are completely off the books.

I choose who, and if, I want to be with someone. I'm not a whore. I'm not doing this for the money. I'm doing it because I like the thrill of it. The excitement of becoming someone else's desire and fantasy. To be wanted so badly by an individual powerful enough to hold half of New York City in his pocket, except when he's in my presence. Then, I'm the one with all the power. I am a prize for the taking, but I decide who the winner is. No, it's not the money I want. I never even ask for money. It's the feeling of being coveted, adored, treasured, if only for a short time. And besides, cheap one night stands that I picked up in bars had gotten old. At least these dates were with rich, sophisticated men who bought me dinner first.

Last night was a regular client, Senator Martin Landon. Dinner with him was never just a standard affair. He always made sure there was another couple at the table with us. His guest was always his personal assistant, Steven Bennett, myself, and another girl from the agency. Usually my friend Faith. Until last night. When I arrived and saw Xander Walker, a *male* escort from the agency, sitting at the table instead, my curiosity was instantly piqued.

What wasn't a convenient detail, was that our dinners were always at the Jean-Georges Mark restaurant, in the Mark Hotel. Where, coincidentally, a suite was in constant reserve for Steven Bennett. No, not the senator. That wouldn't be appropriate at all now, would it? Especially for a man in his position. And like always, after dinner we discreetly made our way to a private elevator that delivered us directly to the suite. Once we were there, Steven would quietly slip away into one of the other rooms, leaving the senator with us.

It was at this point in the evening, the senator would open a bottle of champagne, pour a glass for each of us, and then direct us to the master bedroom. Soft, lusty music was already streaming from hidden speakers, and Faith and I would begin dancing for the senator, our bodies slowly intertwining. The senator would sit in the corner, sipping his champagne, watching our every move, eventually pulling his cock out. He would work it, stroking it with his fist, watching as Faith and I would fall tangled together into the bed. He never joined us. He watched until he came, then he would rise, leave the room, and eventually the suite, not another word said to us. Always a stack of money left behind for us to share.

Until last night. This time, after champagne was poured, after we entered the bedroom and Xander and I began to dance, the senator didn't sit. He removed his jacket, his tie, and loosened the top three buttons of his dress shirt. Martin Landon was a very good looking man in his early forties. The hair just starting to turn a light gray around his temple was the only indicator of his age. He was tall, lean, and handsome with piercing blue eyes that any woman would look twice at. But it dawned on me, the very second he took off his jacket instead of sitting down, that it wasn't a woman he wanted.

My suspicions were confirmed when his eyes zeroed in on Xander's body as he strolled toward us both, his hand latching onto the back of Xander's neck to yank his mouth against his own, unspoken desire exploding. This time when I tumbled into the bed, there were three of us, and the senator did a whole lot more than watch. I passed out shortly after the senator left, sometime after midnight. I chuckled to myself when I realized our dates going forward would be quite different.

My phone dings from somewhere in the next room, and I wonder what time it is. I lift my arm off my face and glance over at the clock. Just a little after nine. A whole new day in front of me. I also work as a registered nurse, and have a shift at the hospital tonight. I think about burying myself under the covers to try and steal a few more hours of rest knowing I'll be up all night, but another ding from my phone changes my mind.

"Who in the actual fuck is texting me at this time of the morning?" I grumble under my breath as I sit up to slide out of the bed. I drag my feet across the soft carpeting, raising my arms to stretch out a long yawn as I enter the main area of the suite.

"Morning slut." A deep voice sounds across the room, startling a yelp from me.

"Jesus fucking Christ, Xander!" I fist my hands on my naked hips. "You scared the shit out of me!"

"Is that why your tits are hard, or are you just happy to see me?" He smirks back at me from the chair he's seated in at the dining room table, a cup of coffee steaming in front of him. Xander is gorgeous. Think Matt Bomer, and then turn it up a few more notches. My eyes dart down to his waist noting the tent starting to appear under the hotel robe he's wearing. He lifts a piece of bacon to his mouth and bites into it, chewing lazily as he stares back at me.

I tilt my head, my lips quirking up into a grin, swinging my hips sexily as I saunter up to him, looking down into his lap. "It looks like I'm not the only one that's happy this morning." I stop in front of him and swing my leg over his lap, lowering myself onto his thighs, sliding my arms around his neck.

"Interested in more than breakfast?" I lean forward and swipe my tongue against his lips teasingly, humming at the salty taste of the bacon. "Yum." He closes the distance between us, crushing his mouth against mine, his tongue sweeping inside to dart against mine, his length hardening completely underneath me. I drag my hands down his chest, spreading the material of the robe open, then grind my hips into his, gliding my wet pussy over his cock.

He chuckles and breaks away. "Didn't get enough last night?"

"I hardly got any last night." I pout, nipping at his bottom lip hungrily. "The senator kept you all to himself."

"Well, let's see if we can fix that." His fingers press into the flesh of my ass as he stands. "Hold on." I tighten my arms around his neck, locking my legs around his waist as he carries me back to the bedroom. He lays me back on the bed, his grip relaxing as he trails a row of soft kisses down my neck, and then lower, latching onto a nipple, sucking it gently. I reach between his legs, find his cock, and begin caressing the silky skin as I pull him toward my center.

He moans, my nipple wet under his hot breath, and steps back. "Condom."

I nod, as he grabs a foil packet off a nearby table, tearing it open. The thin material covers his cock in less than three seconds, his shaft bobbing against his waist as he stalks back to me, eyes dark. "Turn over."

I don't hesitate. I roll and kneel on all fours, arching my ass out to him in an invitation, groaning in bliss when he thrusts inside my pussy in one hard shove. *This*, this is so much better than waking up alone.

Three hours later though, when I wake up again, I am alone. A note on the pillow next to me from Xander confirming just how alone I really am: *Left you half the money. Had fun. ~X*

Ignoring the hollow feeling in my chest, I push myself out of the bed and head to the shower. When I'm done, I find my bag and pull out the oversized t-shirt and leggings I always stow for the morning after. Nothing is worse than pouring yourself back into a dress you wore the night before. Well, maybe dirty panties, but I generally go without, so not a problem there. I place my clothing from the night before in a hotel laundry bag to take with me.

Finally, I sweep the money off the nightstand and count it. Twenty-five hundred dollars. Jesus Christ. That means he left us five thousand dollars. There's something to be said about buying one's silence. Not that it was needed in my case. I don't kiss and tell. End of story.

I take one hundred dollars of the money and put it in my purse for a taxi. I take the rest and seal it in one of the hotel envelopes from the desk in the living room. I put my jacket on, grab my belongings and leave the suite. The doorman flags a taxi for me, and after I'm settled, I give him an address two blocks from my apartment. When we pull up, he turns his head and looks at me with a frown. "This where you wanna go, miss?"

I hand him the hundred. "I've got some sins to repent." I wink. "Keep the change." I'm out of the car before he can object, slamming the door behind me. I sigh as I take in the church looming over me, then climb up the stone steps to the large wooden doors. I pull one open and enter the quiet lobby. The smell of old wax and cinnamon scented incense greets me as I make my way to the prayer candles located on one side of the pews. There are two people seated in the benches, each a row apart, but other than that, the place is empty.

I grasp one of the lighting sticks and hold it over one of the already lit candles until it flames, then I light a new candle. I lift the stick to my lips and blow softly, extinguishing the flame before placing the stick back in its metal holder. I pull the envelope out of my jacket pocket, lift the lid of the offering box, and drop it inside. I do this quickly, knowing the envelope won't fit into the slot, then turn on my heel and exit the church like my hair is on fire. Once I'm back on the sidewalk, I slow my gait and stroll the two blocks to my building at a leisurely pace, the doorman greeting me as I enter.

I take the elevator to the twelfth floor, stepping out when it arrives, unlocking the door before I walk through into the apartment. I drop my purse and the laundry bag onto the floor, sighing loudly, the sound echoing across the large space, reminding me how empty it is. I glance at my wrist for the time, a little after two. Only five hours until my shift starts at the hospital. Five hours of silence and solitude. I can handle that…

CHAPTER Two

~Cameron~

"One scoop or two, squirt?" I plunge the large spoon I'm holding into a carton of ice cream.

"Three, daddy!" My beautiful daughter sits up on her knees, bouncing while she claps her hands. "I want three!"

Smiling, I plop the first spoonful into the bowl in front of me and chuckle. "How about two? Mommy won't be very happy if I send you home all sugared up."

This earns me a dramatic eye roll, alarmingly diva-like, which at six-years-old, gives me a slight pause of fear. *These are supposed to be the easy years.* "Daddy, it's no big deal."

"It will be when I drop you off in an hour and Mommy yells at me, so two scoops it is." The second spoonful splats on top of the first in the bowl, accompanied by a loud sigh from across the counter. "Whatever."

"Willow." I glower in her direction, my message clear to her with one glance.

"Sorry, daddy." She mumbles, sitting back on her feet.

I grab the syrup sitting next to the ice cream, pop the cover and begin drizzling it generously over the ice cream. A large grin lifts my cheeks as I peer over the bottle at her. "Besides, with all this chocolate, who needs three scoops?"

Her eyes jump up to my mine, sparkling with delight once again, her face glowing in appreciation, as she nods her approval. "Thank you, daddy!"

"You're welcome, my little bean." I slide the bowl in front of her, grabbing a smaller spoon from the drawer at my waist, and give her that as well. "Dig in."

A warm feeling spreads across my chest at the extreme joy she exudes over the simplicity of a bowl of ice cream. This child has absolutely no idea how much she's adored, by both her mother and me, even if we do it living apart now. One corner of my mouth pulls down at that thought, but only for the briefest of moments. While there was a time our being together was blissful, that time ended several years ago.

I put the ice cream fixings away in their respective places, then come around the counter to drop a kiss onto Willow's braided hair. "I'm going to change and then we'll head out to drop you back off at Mommy's, okay?"

"Do I have to go back already?" Her spoon clatters against the side of the bowl as she turns to look up at me.

"Afraid so. Daddy's got to work tonight and you've got

school tomorrow." I point to her bowl. "Finish up and I'll be out in just a few minutes."

Her head bobs in response as I turn and walk the short distance to my bedroom. When my ex, Indigo, and I divorced two years ago, I moved into a small, two-bedroom apartment on the edge of Harlem. She moved into her then-lover, now husband's three-million-dollar co-op on the Upper West Side. I couldn't really blame her for our divorce. I was too busy trying to get ahead at the department, instead of spending time with her and Willow. When I realized what I had lost, it was too late. Her new husband is good to Willow, and good to Indigo too, so I'm happy for them. I spend every other weekend with Willow, and any day off in my schedule that allows for it. Not ideal, but not terrible either.

I change into a pair of nylon athletic pants, and a t-shirt, then slide my feet into a pair of running shoes. I packed my work suit and shoes earlier, so grab the garment bag off the hook on my closet door and head out to the kitchen to the sound of running water.

Willow stands on her tip toes as she reaches up to turn the faucet off. Sneaking behind her, I grasp her waist, hoisting her up and around to squeeze her in my arms. "You washed your own bowl?" I smother her neck in kisses. "You're the best daughter a daddy could have."

Her soft palms land on both cheeks as she holds my face. "And you're the best daddy a daughter could have."

We both smile as I lean forward to press a kiss to the tip of her button nose. "I love you Willow Bean."

"I love you too, Daddy Bear." She returns the kiss to the

tip of my nose, and I give her one more soft hug before setting her on her feet.

"Okay, let's grab your backpack and hit the road."

Twenty minutes later, I drop Willow off with her mom in front of their co-op on West Eighty-First Street, then head straight for Central Park West, sliding into an open space next to the Hayden Planetarium. One of the perks of having a police-issued vehicle; parking just about anywhere in the city without the fear of being towed. Even though it's an unmarked car, it's got police plates, so I know I'm safe. I glance down at my watch and note the time. It's just a little after five, but the sky is already beginning to darken. I'll be happy in another week when we can turn the clocks ahead and the days stay lighter a bit longer.

I always try and get a run in before my shift, and on the days I drop Willow off, I run in Central Park. I'll do a loop, taking Seventy-Ninth Avenue through the park, past Belvedere Castle, until I hit Fifth Avenue. From there I run North along the entire length of the MET before turning West again on Eighty-Sixth, cutting back through the park, past the Jackie O Reservoir, until I'm back on Central Park West again.

I step out of the car and wonder if the hoodie I have on will be enough to keep me warm. I shrug to no one particular, knowing it will have to do because I don't have anything else besides my wool trench coat in the car. I jog across the main road to enter the park, then pick up my gait until I'm running at a good pace. I leave my phone in the car when I run, preferring to listen to the sounds in the park, instead of music, knowing my head will be swarming with all kinds of noise once I start my shift.

It's quieter than usual tonight, I assume the cool temperature and early darkness keeping people off the usually busy path, my feet slapping against the pavement the only sound. My breath is puffing out in bursts of white clouds with every other footfall, my stride reaching a nice rhythm by the time I'm almost to the castle. I cock my head toward a movement I catch out of the corner of my eye, screeching to a halt when I hear something. I try and quiet my breathing as I turn and walk toward the motion I think I saw, my heart rate accelerating I hear someone call out again.

"Help me." It's hoarse, but there's no mistaking the cry.

I break into a sprint, sliding down onto the ground as I reach the sound of the voice, my knees almost crashing into a form huddled in a ball on the grass. "Are you hurt?" I reach out to touch the person, and they flinch away from me, curling deeper into themselves.

"Please don't hurt me." The terror-filled voice begs.

"I'm Detective Cameron Justice with the New York Police Department." I hold my hands open wide so the person can see I'm not going to hurt them. "Have you been hurt? Can I help you?"

The ball before me unfurls slowly to reveal a badly beaten young woman, her face bloody and swollen, her clothes shredded. "Please help me." Her body is shaking violently, so I rip my sweatshirt over my head and hold it out to her.

"Let me help put this on you, okay?" She nods her head, and I pull it as gently as I can over her small, battered form. "Are you alone?"

She nods her head, tears streaming down her cheeks like an open faucet. "I— I was attacked."

My nostrils flare as I grind my teeth, trying my best to hide my outrage. Of all the damn times to not have my phone with me. I hold my hand out to the girl. "Can you walk? Let's get you out of here."

She tries to stand, her knees shaking so badly she crumples in a heap before me, howling in anguish. I notice her feet are bare and wonder who the fuck did this to her, my jaw clenching silently. I blow out a breath to calm myself and bend in front of her, keeping my voice gentle and low. "Will you let me carry you?" Tear streaked cheeks peer up at me, her head bopping up and down. I slide my arms tenderly around her and then sweep her up, cradling her delicately against the warmth of my chest. "I won't hurt you." I murmur quietly into her hair as I walk quickly back toward the direction I came in. "I have a squad car just off the CPW. Let's get you there and get you warm."

Her body is limp in my arms, but the slight nod of her head tells me she's still conscious. I try and talk to her to keep her calm. "Can you tell me your name?"

"Cindy." She whispers. "Cindy Morrison."

"Do you know who did this to you?" I ask softly.

She whimpers, shaking her head. "It was a john. He said he just wanted a quick blow. He said he would pay me fifty dollars."

She was a prostitute. *Great, that just made this that much harder.* On her. Because no one would see a prostitute being beaten as a crime. But to me it was. Anyone being beaten was wrong. I didn't care who they were. No one deserved to be beaten the way this girl obviously had been.

"Okay, Cindy. We're almost to the car." I almost jolt in

horror when we finally step under a street light and see the full extent of her injuries. Whoever did this to her is going to pay. I wait for a break in the traffic and jog across the street, her broken body trembling in my arms as I reach my car and place her on the hood. "I just need to unlock the car."

I make sure I tell her everything I'm doing so I won't scare her. I fish the keys out of the zippered pocket of my pants to unlock the car, yanking the back door open. "Cindy, I'm going to put you in the back seat, okay?"

She nods her head, as I slide my hands under her, lifting her gently from the hood and into the back seat. I reach across the seat and pull my wool trench over her body to help warm her. "Okay, let's get you to a hospital."

I slide into the front seat, start the car, and turn the heat up high. I grab my phone and call my precinct, the phone ringing as I pull my car into traffic, activating the lights and siren as I go.

"Fourteenth Precinct, Detective Sawyer speaking."

"Sawyer, it's Justice."

"You in pursuit or something?" He could obviously hear the siren.

"Found a beaten girl while I was running through the park. On the southwest side of the castle, about fifty feet off the path. Get a team over there. I have her. I'm taking her to a hospital."

"Okay, you got it. Which hospital?"

"University. It's the closest with a trauma center. Have Nolan meet me there when he gets in."

"I'll let him know. Keep us updated."

"Yep." I end the call and glance in the rearview to check

on Cindy. "You doing okay back there?" She nods her head but doesn't speak, one eye almost swollen shut. "We're almost there." I press down on the accelerator and weave through the rush-hour traffic in an attempt to keep my word.

CHAPTER
Three

~Gabrielle~

"Can I get some help here?" A deep, male voice shouts from the lobby.

My head snaps up, pulling my attention away from the form I'm filling out, my body rising automatically from my chair. My eyes lock onto the limp form being carried through the doors by a tall man. I press the button to open the doors to the unit and wave him through. "Is she breathing?"

"Yes, but she's been badly beaten."

"Follow me." I lead him out of the trauma room and down the hall, pointing to an empty bed in the first room we approach. "Please, place her there." I step outside the room, look down the hall for Trey, the Physician Assistant on duty tonight, but don't see him, so I step back inside and to the bedside.

"Hi, I'm Nurse Reed, but you can call me Gabby." I rest my hand gently over the trembling girl's fingers. "I'm going to help you, okay?" She nods. "Can you tell me your name?"

"Cin-Cindy." She stutters out, her body shaking horribly.

"Cindy, I'll be right back." I pat her hand. "I'm just going to get you a warm blanket." I address the man standing next to her. "Are you okay with her for a minute?"

He nods. "Yes."

I turn on my heel, rush down the hallway, spot Trey with another patient, and stop just outside the doorway, peeking my head in. "Excuse me, Trey?"

He turns. "Yes?"

"Room one when you can, please." He nods and I move again, walking further down the hall to the warming cart, pulling two blankets out. I charge back to Cindy, relieved when I see Kinsley, one of the other nurses working with me that evening, in the room.

"Here you go, this should help." I unfold the warm blankets over her shivering form and tuck them around her body to hold in the heat. I turn my attention to Kinsley. "You got this?"

"Sure do." She gives me a warm smile, then turns toward the male. "Why don't you go with Nurse Reed? Help her with any information she needs to check Cindy in."

That was Kinsley's polite way of asking the man to get the hell out of the room so she could take care of the patient properly. And to find out if he was the cause of her injuries. Because honestly, we've seen it plenty of times before. A husband beats his wife, then an hour later, feeling remorseful, brings her to the hospital to be treated, for a *'fall down the stairs'*.

His brow furrows as he glances back and forth at us. "Sure, no problem." He follows me out of the room, as I lead him to the privacy of the triage room, where patients are normally checked in. I'm on intake tonight, so lucky me, I get to find out what supposedly happened.

I sit and offer him a chair. "Please, have a seat." He takes the chair against the wall, picks it up, then puts it down a foot away from me. My brow arches in surprise as he sits, his knee inches from mine. "Make yourself comfortable." I stated dryly.

He smirks, shaking his head. "I'm Detective Justice, Fourteenth Precinct. I encountered the victim this evening and brought her here in my car."

Shit. Guess I called this one wrong. Not that I'm going to let him off that easy. "Do you have a badge? Because you're looking a little casual tonight detective." *Casual yes, but damn, those arms of his were looking mighty fine in that t-shirt.*

He blinks, a slow breath blowing from his nostrils before he speaks. "I was jogging. In Central Park. Before my shift. I found her crumbled in a heap off of one the paths. Didn't really have time to change." He stands, my neck craning back to take in his full height. "I'd be happy to go get my badge out of the car for you."

I rise, only coming up to his chin. I'm tall at five-feet ten-inches, so guess he's easily over six feet. *Tall and nicely built. Oh, and apparently not a woman beater.* "That would be great actually." I press the button to release the door, and nod in its direction, making it obvious he can go.

He scoffs, then walks toward the exit, throwing a parting

glance over his shoulder in my direction as he does. "Be right back."

"I'll be here." The corners of my mouth lifting in a mock grin. "With bells on." My gaze travels down the length of his long, muscled frame, pausing on his firm backside as he pushes through the exit door. He's all man, from head to toe, and I hum in appreciation. He's back in less than five minutes, a garment bag slung over one shoulder, a badge dangling around his neck on a metal chain, and a look of smug satisfaction on his face. *Bastard.*

"Happy now?" His eyes narrowing as he locks his gaze with mine as he strolls back inside the triage room.

"Ecstatic." I drawl. "Going to the prom after?" I tilt my head toward the garment bag.

He smirks. "You're a damn ball-buster. Anyone ever tell you that?"

I try, unsuccessfully, to hide my matching smirk, and laugh instead, breaking the tension. "Once or twice."

"We *are* on the same side." He drapes the bag over the chair he was sitting in before, then crosses his arms, drawing my attention to the muscled grooves in his forearms. "At least, I think we are."

I lift my gaze to meet his and smile graciously in defeat, nodding once. "We are." I shift to lean a hip against the counter. "We're just very protective of our patients."

"Let's start over." He holds a hand out in front of me. "I'm Cameron Justice, nice to meet you."

My cheeks rise even higher as my smile widens, and I slip my hand into his. My stomach clenches when he wraps his fingers around mine, warm electricity zapping up my arm. I know he feels it too because his eyes widened for just a second, and instead of letting go, his grip tightens. I blink, a whoosh of air leaving my lips as I reply. "Gabby Reed."

We stare at each other, locked in some kind of invisible trance, my hand still in his, for maybe five seconds or maybe five minutes. I'm not sure because it feels like time comes to a complete standstill around us until we're interrupted. "Justice, you copying me?"

His grip releases its tender hold, my hand feeling cool at the loss of his touch, both of our heads turning to the person speaking. "Earth to Justice."

"Jesus, Nolan, I heard you the first time." Cameron wipes his hand down the back of his shaved head, then turns back to me. "This is my partner, Brian Nolan. Can you let him in?"

"Oh, sure." I reach for the switch on the wall and push it, the lock buzzing, the door swinging open as his partner steps inside the space with us.

"What, you're not going to ask him for his badge?" Cameron teases, one side of his mouth crooking up into a smile.

I arch a brow and sweep my hand up the length of Brian's torso. "No, because he actually looks like a cop."

Brian tilts his head down, inspecting his blue, button-up shirt, tucked into dark, grey trousers. He smoothes his hand down his tan trench coat, before looking back up in question. "Is it that obvious?"

I shrug my shoulders. "It could be the gun holstered to your side."

He pats the butt of the gun, then looks down at his clothing again before lifting his eyes back to us. "Cause the outfit's okay, right?"

This earns him a dramatic eye roll from his partner. "Christ Nolan, who the hell cares about your outfit?"

"Well, me." He tugs at the lapels of the coat. "I work hard at this look."

"Listen, if you boys are done talking fashion, I'd love to get this paperwork taken care of." Both heads twist in my direction.

"Sorry." They respond, then grimace as they look at each other.

"Someone want to catch me up?" Brian changes the subject.

"Why don't you two talk, and I'll go check on Cindy?" I offer.

"Who's Cindy?" Brian scratches his temple.

"The victim," Cameron replies, exasperation lacing his tone.

"The patient." I retort sharply, cutting him off before he can finish, tossing them both a hard glance. "I'll be back." I turn on my heel before I'm caught up in another conversation with them, and head toward the patient rooms. I run into Trey in the hallway and stop. "How is she?"

"Just went up to x-ray." His lips clench into a tight line. "Probably a cracked orbital lobe, a broken nose, and maybe some ribs as well. She's going to be pretty sore for a while."

"Was she raped?" My voice is low, almost afraid of the answer.

"She said she wasn't. Refused a cervical exam." He shakes his head. "I'm honestly not sure if she was or not. I did get scrapings from under her fingernails, not that it may even matter. She's already asking when she can leave."

"She's scared of someone or something then." I frown. "Are you discharging her?"

"Nope. Keeping her overnight. She's going to be too sore to go anywhere tonight."

"There are detectives here that would like to talk to her."

A scowl darkens Trey's features. "I know they're trying to help, but could they at least give her a chance to get treated?"

"I'll tell them it's going to be at least a half-hour so you can get her comfortable when she's back from x-ray."

He nods. "Sounds good. Thanks, Gabs." We part, both of us walking back in the direction we came from.

When I enter the triage room, Brian is sitting in one of the chairs, scrolling through his phone, and Cameron is gone. "Hey." Brian's attention switching to me. "She's in x-ray right now. It's probably going to be at least another half-hour before you can speak to her."

He pushes himself out of the chair to stand in front of me. "Okay." He looks out the clear glass behind me then back at me. "Cameron went to change. I'll go find him and maybe hit the cafeteria." He points to the buzzer in a silent request, which I reply by pressing. "We'll come back in a bit."

He starts walking out the door just as Cameron rounds the corner, and holy shit, he looks like a completely different man. His frame is now covered in a dark, navy suit, definitely tailored to fit his toned frame because it falls perfectly on him. The crisp, white shirt tucked into the slacks is in stark contrast to his cocoa colored skin, only enhancing his handsome features. One side of his mouth slides up in what can only be described as cocky when he catches me staring unabashedly. When he's two feet in front of me, he glides to a stop, one brow arching high. "Does this meet your detective dress code?"

Recovering quickly, my insides warming at just how delicious he looks, I lean over the counter, closer to him, smiling coyly, as I flirt brazenly. "Oh, you meet *all* kinds of dress codes."

He tilts his head, chuckling at my compliment. "Glad to finally have your approval on something." He points behind me. "Can I press my luck and question the vict-, sorry, the patient next?"

"She's in x-ray." I nod toward his partner. "I was just telling Brian it's going to be at least another half-hour. If you guys have something else you need to do, or if you want to get something in the cafeteria, you have some time to kill. The food's actually not that bad."

"Okay." He motions to Brian. "Let's go get a coffee and check in with the team at the scene."

"Sounds good." Brian walks out into the waiting area, turning to see if Cameron's following.

He's not. He's looking back at me, eyes laser-focused on mine. I hold his stare for ten seconds before breaking. "Can I help you with something else?"

"Go out to dinner with me." I think it's supposed to be a question, but I love that it didn't come out like one.

"We don't even like each other." I scoff, challenging him.

Instead of backing down, he takes a step closer, only inches from me now, his voice low when he speaks. "I'm trained to know when someone is lying." His eyes shift to my lips, which involuntarily smirk, then trail slowly back up to my eyes. "And I know you want to say yes."

"You think you've got me all figured out already, huh?" I push my weight off the counter, putting a little space between us. He tracks my movement with his eyes but doesn't move an inch.

"I think you're as curious about me as I am about you." He leans a fraction closer. "Just say yes."

"Yes." I surprise even myself when the word bursts from my lips, and I take an abrupt step back, my posture going rigid, eliciting a low chuckle from him. *What the hell have I just gotten myself into?*

CHAPTER Four

~Cameron~

It's Thursday; four days since I asked Gabby Reed on a date. I've been wracking my brain the entire time, trying to come up with a cool place to take her, but so far I'd come up with diddly squat. And I'm supposed to be picking her up in just a couple hours. I wasn't concerned until she gave me her address; apartment 12R, at The Pierre, on Fifth Avenue. *Who the hell lives on Fifth Avenue?* No one I know, that's for sure. And how the hell can someone who works as a nurse afford to live there?

She didn't seem like a high maintenance kind of girl at the hospital. Her dark hair was twisted up in a messy bun on her head, and she was wearing plain old blue hospital scrubs. Not Louis Viton or some fancy, designer brand. I did notice she had a nice watch on; a Cartier Tank to be exact, but it could have been a gift, or even a knock off. I was doubting the knock off option now that I knew her address.

We'd been texting flirty banter back and forth over the last few days as well, and nothing screamed 'snob'. I flip open my laptop and open Google, then type *unique places to bring a date in Manhattan* and hit search. I drum my fingers lightly on the table as I browse the top ten responses returned.

1. **Take a Tarot Reading Class**

Absolutely not. I'll either up end being told the end is near, or all my dreams are about to
come true. Either way, I can get that bullshit anytime I'm in China Town if I want.

1. **Take a Peek at the Museum of Interesting Things**

Maybe I should have typed, unique places to bring a date in Manhattan if you're a cop, because I see more than enough interesting things every night I'm on duty.

1. **Take a Graffiti Lesson**

This was getting better and better. I scrub my hand down my face and slam the laptop shut. Why is this so god damn difficult? It's certainly not the first date I've gone on since my divorce. It's not like me to let any kind of social status get in the way of taking control of a situation and rolling with it. Was I letting the black boy from Harlem, takes out a rich white girl stereotype get under my skin? Screw that. I was way better than that. My phone dings, interrupting the conversation I'm having with myself, and I grab it off the table, reading the text.

~How should I dress? Is seven still good?

Was she reading my damn mind from across town? I make a decision right then. I'm not going to do anything special or different to try and impress this woman. She was either going to like me for who I was, or she wasn't. I'd bring her to my favorite place to eat and if she snubbed her nose up, that would tell me everything I would need to know. I type in my reply and hit send.

~Dress casual. See you at seven.

She replies instantly.

~I'll be waiting with bells on.

Damn, she just loves to bust my balls. Thinking of her this week actually did something else to my balls, and just that thought alone causes my cock to throb. I stand, shifting my junk as I do, and glance at the clock. It's just after five, and decide there's no better time to jump in the shower; a cold one to be safe. Fifteen minutes later, I wrap a towel around my waist and exit the bathroom, walking across the hall into my bedroom. I step into a pair of dark colored jeans, then shrug a light blue shirt over my shoulders, buttoning it up.

I really want to throw my favorite ball cap on too, but figure for a first date, I better not go quite that casual. I spray a little cologne on and search for a pair of matching dark socks in the laundry basket sitting in front of my dresser. When I finally strike gold, I slide them over my feet, then reach from my ankle holster. I strap the holster around my right leg, then slide my Glock 9mm inside, adjusting my pant leg to cover the gun. Not the most common accessory on a date, but one I refuse to go without in my line of work. And what she doesn't know, hopefully, won't be a problem.

The days are starting to get a little warmer, but at night it gets chilly again, so I pull on a leather coat and wrap a gray scarf around my neck as I walk out the door. It's only six, but getting to mid-town on a Thursday night is no easy feat. It would be so much better if I could move closer, but rental costs are absurd, so a shitty commute is something I have to deal with.

When I'm about twenty minutes out, my phone pings, alerting me to a text message. At the next red light, I read the text.

~Having a drink in the bar. Just text when you arrive and I'll come out.

I don't text her back. I kind of like the idea of making her wonder a little bit, especially knowing that with today's technology, she'll be able to see that I've read the message. Besides, there's no way I'm picking her up on the curb like a god damn hooker. I'll go in and pick her up like a gentleman.

When I arrive at her building, I pull up to the curb next to the valet service and shake my head in disbelief. What kind of person lives in a hotel? I'm baffled and intrigued all at the same time. I step out of the vehicle and greet the uniformed gentleman already waiting for me.

"Good evening, sir. Valet?"

"I'm actually just picking someone up. Shouldn't be long."

He glances at the car, the uniform dark blue sedan a dead giveaway for all New York City undercover police, then back at me, a tight smile appearing. "Of course, no problem officer."

"It's detective." I leave it at that, letting him wonder if I'm here to arrest one of the elite clients that frequent here, instead of my actual purpose, and stroll through the revolving door into the lobby. The lobby isn't as grand as I was expecting, the floor checkered in white and black marble, with a long reception counter against the wall. A concierge desk sits to one side, and I ask the person working behind it where the bar is.

I find it easily enough and see my target as soon as I step into the room. She's seated at the bar, her body angled so that I can see her side profile. The first thing I notice is how beautiful she looks with her hair down. It's much longer than I would have guessed, falling in soft waves halfway down the back of the soft white sweater she's wearing. She's talking to the bartender, her lips, tinted a light red, tilted up in a smile. She's got one long, black leather clad leg crossed over the other, a suede knee-high boot with a three-inch heel bouncing lightly.

One side of my mouth quirks up when I see her glance down at her phone, no doubt checking for a text from me. I drift in her direction, like a moth to a flame, almost expecting her to be hot to the touch when I place my hand on her shoulder.

Her face swings to mine, her mouth forming a small circle, eyes widening momentarily before crinkling around the edges as a smile forms. "Cameron!"

"Gabby." I release her shoulder to slide my hand down her arm until my fingers wrap softly around hers, the same tingling feeling I felt the last time we touched, zapping through me again.

"You didn't have to come in." She rushes out, her cheeks turning the softest shade of pink as she glimpses at our entwined fingers. "I could have met you outside."

"I didn't mind coming in." I reluctantly release my hold on her to sit on the stool next to her, my eyes trailing down the length of her body, then tracking slowly up until my gaze locks with hers. "You look stunning."

She lifts the glass tumbler gripped in her other hand to her lips and takes a slow sip, peering over the rim, her eyes raking down my frame. She lowers the glass back to the bar, her tongue sneaking out to capture some of the moisture on her lip. My cock throbs in response, and I shift in the stool, pulling my jacket closed.

"Well, you certainly do not look like a detective tonight." Her finger tracing lazily around the rim of the glass as she continues to stare at me, a sexy smirk on her lips. "Not that I'm complaining."

"Mission accomplished then." I chuckle softly, then point to her glass. "Are you finished?"

She brings the glass to her mouth and drains what's left in one swallow, the ice cubes clinking as she places it back on the bar, smiling wide. "Yep."

We stand at the same time, our bodies colliding in the tight space. Her hair swings around my face, the soft tresses skimming over my skin, the subtle scent of coconut floating up into my nostrils. Her fingers dig into my bicep at the same time her breasts press into my chest, our eyes meeting as my hand wraps around her waist to steady us.

"Oh!" Her breathe warm against my skin, the faint smell of tequila on her lips.

"I got you." I stare back at her, then blink, murmuring. "Your eyes are like a mermaid's tail."

Her brow furrows, her lips lifting in a small smile. "What?"

"Your eyes." I tilt my head as I stare into them. "They aren't one color. They are blue, and green, and grey, almost speckled. Like a mermaid's tail would look like in the sun."

Her cheeks lift as her face brightens into a wide smile. "That may be one of the nicest things anyone has ever said about my eyes." She laughs. "Definitely the most original."

"Blame it on having a six-year-old daughter who's obsessed with The Little Mermaid." I shrug, smiling.

Her brows shoot up and she steps sideways, my hold on her waist severed as she does. "You have a child?"

I grip the back of my neck, tilting my head as I absorb the shock on her face. "Is that a problem?" I release the hold on my neck to rub my hand up the back of my head. I guess it's better to know right now if she doesn't like children. No time wasted this way.

She sweeps her hair behind one ear and then plants her hand on one hip. "Are you married?"

I scoff and take a step closer, wanting to keep my voice low. "Do I seem like the kind of man that would ask you out on a date if I was married?"

"You wouldn't be the first." She hisses. "And cops are the worst cheaters of them all. Telling their wives they're on duty when they're actually out screwing around on them." Her hands are fisted on both hips now.

I shake my head in disbelief. "Jesus, someone sure did a

number on you." I cross my arms as I continue, "but I can tell you right now, that's not the kind of man I am."

She takes a step closer, her teeth practically grinding when she speaks. "Not me. My friend Charlie. Twice." She holds up two fingers. "Two separate times, both times cops, fucking cheating on their wives. Do you know how devastated she was when she found out? She is the sweetest, most loving person I know, and the idea that she had any part in the deception in someone's marriage wrecked her."

"Listen, I'm sorry that happened to your friend, but that's not me. I'm divorced. Almost two years. My ex is happily remarried to someone else." I find myself softening after hearing her so fiercely defend her concerns based on her friend's bad luck. I step forward to reach for her hand, grasping it softly in mine. "Gabby, I swear to you, on my daughter, I'm single."

"What's her name?" She asks after several seconds, her hand relaxing in mine. "Your daughter?"

"Willow." I smile at the very thought of her. "I call her my little Willow-Bean. I tell her she's like my very own little Beanie Baby."

"That's sweet." She looks down at her feet then back up at me. "I'm sorry if I over-reacted."

"Apology accepted." My thumb grazes back and forth over the soft skin of her palm before I release her hand and nod toward the bar. "Let me pay for your drink and we can go."

"Oh, no." She waves my offer away. "It's all set. I have a house account here."

"So, you actually live here? In this hotel?" I have to ask.

Maybe it's the detective in me, but I'm curious as hell about it.

"My parents own a residence here." She shrugs as we walk out of the lounge toward the lobby. "They rarely come to the city. They have a house in Bridgeport, and prefer to stay there most of the time."

"A house in Bridgeport, and an apartment in a hotel that faces Central Park." I blow out a long breath. "So, you're rich."

She stops in the hallway, turning to look at me. She's wearing heels, and almost as tall as me in them, so her eyes are level with mine. "My parents are rich."

"But you live off the spoils of those riches?" I ask, not trying to challenge her, just trying to understand.

"I work. I make my own money." She sighs, shrugging. "But yes, I live here for free, I have a trust fund, and credit cards that my father pays for. I'm their only child. They don't know any other way except to keep taking care of me."

"Okay."

"That's it?" She raises a brow as she cocks her head. "Just like that? No being intimidated by the poor, little, rich girl?"

"Nope." I step, closing the distance between us to slide a hand through her silky waves to grip onto the back of her head and press my lips against hers. Her hands glide around my neck as I tug her closer, her body relaxing against mine as our kiss deepens. I break away, capturing her lips one more time before I release her completely, my eyes on hers. "Not even a little bit."

She laughs. "Good, because I think I'm beginning to actually like you."

I start walking again, placing my hand on her lower

back, not wanting to separate completely from her. "Told ya so." Referring to the fact that I already noted this at the hospital the night we met.

We reach the lobby, and she asks me to wait just a moment while she gets her coat from one of the bellmen. He's back in less than thirty seconds and helps her into it. I tilt my head, my brow raised as she struts back to me, looking even more gorgeous in the mid-length white fur coat she's now wearing. She shakes a finger at me as she approaches, a cute grin on her face. "Don't even say it."

I hold my hands up in surrender, chuckling. "Wouldn't dream of it." I snag her hand back in mine as we head to the exit. "But I did say casual."

"This is my casual." She defends.

"Noted, and good to know." I chuckle again. "You hungry? Want to eat?"

"Starving actually." She growls back.

"Mexican, okay?" I release her hand so we can push through the revolving door. "There's a place I love on the other side of the park."

"I like any place that serves tequila." She grins widely, her step faltering when I stop in front of my car, still parked right where I left it. She looks at the car, then at me. "You're seriously taking me on a date in your cop car?"

"Not fancy enough for you, poor little rich girl?" I joke, opening the passenger door for her.

"We can take the car service here?" She suggests, not getting into the car. "You know, in case you want to drink? They can return us here, after."

"I'll be fine, but thanks." I shoot her an exaggerated wink. "Now get your pampered ass in the car princess."

"Can we at least play with the siren?" She jokes as she slides gracefully into the seat.

"Only if you let me handcuff you first." I quip.

She holds her wrists out, her voice dropping an octave. "Lock me up already."

She's peeking seductively up at me under her lashes, and I realize she's not kidding in the least. My cock throbs in protest when I shut the door on her suggestion. *What the hell have I just gotten myself into?*

CHAPTER
Five

~Gabrielle~

I watch as he walks around the front of the car, then pauses a moment before he pulls the door open to slide behind the wheel of the car. Perhaps he's as unsettled as I am right now. I honestly would be perfectly fine with forfeiting dinner for some time under his lock and key. I think he's hell bent on being a perfect gentleman, unfortunately for me, so I stow my dirty thoughts and fold my hands in my lap.

He reaches over his shoulder for his seat belt, pulling it across his chest, clicking the lock into place. He stares at me for a minute, then frowns. "Are you going to put your seat belt on?"

I cover my mouth with my fingers to try and hide my smile. "Really?" I'm usually in taxi's, Uber's, or the car service, and never even think to wear it, so the request from him seems silly.

"Yes, really." He leans over me to snatch the belt, pulling it over my chest and across my waist, buckling it in place. I inhale deeply, savoring the clean woodsy smell of him. "Do you know how many accidents there are on a nightly basis around here?"

I shake my head, trying not to laugh. "No." I wrap a hand around the strap resting across my chest to give it a tug. "But looks like I'm good and safe now. Thanks, Dad." I lift the corner of my lips as I turn to him. "This isn't exactly what I had in mind when I suggested you lock me up."

His grey eyes melt into liquid platinum as he tilts closer. "But this is infinitely safer." He brushes a chaste kiss against my cheek, chuckling. "For me, I think." He straightens his spine against the seat, starts the car, and gives me a wide smile as he pulls out onto Fifth Avenue. He takes the Sixty-Fifth Transverse through the park, cutting our travel time by more than half, and within fifteen minutes we're pulling into a parking spot on Seventy-Seventh Avenue. We get extremely lucky, a car exiting a spot just seconds before we arrive.

He opens the door, extending his hand to help me out of the car. A small bolt of electricity shoots down my arm when he twines his fingers with mine, my pulse quickening as a result. I obviously go on a lot of dates in my *other* line of work, but no one, and I mean no one, has ever held my hand. It's such a minuscule thing in the big scope of things, but my heart flutters like a baby bird trying to find its wings.

We walk together to the entrance of the restaurant, him pulling the large, carved wooden door open for me to enter, his fingers never leaving mine. I lean my body into his, this tiny feeling of possession by him softening my standard jagged edges.

An older woman, silver hair pulled up in a loose bun on the top of her head, wearing a bright, traditional Mexican dress claps her hands in delight when she spots Cameron. "Senor Justice! We have not seen you in weeks!" She comes around the hostess station and brings her plump hands to his face, dragging him down to her height as she kisses him on both cheeks. "We have missed you!" She clucks before turning her attention in my direction, her eyes growing wide. "And is this the cause? Ohhh, dios mío!" She clutches onto my free hand, lifting it as she inspects me before looking at Cameron. "She is hermosa, eh senor?" She waggles her brows. "Si. I understand now why you have stayed away."

Cameron's head falls back as a belly full of laughter erupts, his body shaking, eliciting my own fit of giggles over the whole spectacle. He's clearly a regular, and a well-liked one. "Si, Senora Graciela, es muy bonito, y tengo el fallo tu usted tambien." My eyes pop wide, my mouth falling slightly open as he speaks to her in fluent Spanish. This guy is full of surprises, and so far, they are all amazing. He switches back to English as he pulls me forward slightly. "This is Senora Gabby."

She's still holding my hand and gives it a gentle hug as she stands on tiptoe to press a dry kiss to my cheek. "Nice to meet you lovely girl." She lowers herself, her face brightening with a large, toothy smile as she nods her head. "You want dinner then, si senor?"

"Si, por favor." He nods back at her.

"Come my friends." She grabs two menus from the stand and waves her hand to follow. She seats us at a table in the far corner, next to a window. "I'll bring you both the tortilla soup to start. It's excellent tonight." She scurries off, without even waiting for a response.

"She's a little firecracker." I remark, opening one of the menus.

"She's got a heart of gold." He's staring in her direction, his eyes soft, then switches his attention back to me. He reaches over to slides the menu out of my hold. "Trust me?"

Lord knows I've given up a lot more than what to have for dinner when it comes to choices, so I nod. "Absolutely."

A waitress appears and after greeting her, he orders two Frida's, no salt, and an order of guacamole and chips, no cilantro, at my request. A second after she leaves, a different server arrives to place two steaming bowls of soup in front of us, freshly grated cheese melting into the tomato-based broth. My mouth waters as I lift my spoon to take a taste. I hum, loudly. "Oh my god, this is amazing!"

"Everything here is out of this world. Wait until you try the guac." He grins, taking a bite of the soup. Our drinks arrive, and then shortly after, our chips and guacamole.

"So, tell me about yourself." He scoops up some of the green yumminess onto a chip and stuffs it into his mouth.

"Ugh." I roll my eyes.

"What?" His eyebrows slant together as he frowns. "Not a good subject?"

"Just boring." I shrug. "You already know I've got rich parents, am an only child, and work as a nurse. Everything else you see, is pretty much what you get with me. I'd rather hear about you."

He chuckles. "Okay, what do you want to know?"

"Where do you live? What happened between you and your wife? How long have you been a detective? Any brothers or sisters? How come your eyes are grey? Do you put out on the first date?"

I take a large gulp of my margarita trying to hide the smirk on my face, as his eyes bulge on my last question. It's always more fun to toss my intentions out in the open.

"Damn woman, you don't waste time, do you?" He licks his lips before taking his own fortifying gulp of courage from his drink.

"Life is way too short for that." I tilt my head coyly. "I don't believe in wasting time, and I think it's more than obvious that we're into each other."

He snorts, grinning. "I knew you were going to be trouble."

"Only the good kind." I tease. "I promise."

"There's no good kind of trouble." He takes another drink from his glass. "I'm a cop, remember? I've seen it all."

I stare back at him, the tequila making me braver than usual. "So, what, you just want to be friends?"

"Yes, it's a good place to start, don't you think?" He reaches over the table and snags my hand in his, locking his eyes with mine. "Not going to lie, Gabby. You're gorgeous, and I'm insanely attracted to you, but if I just wanted to get laid, I wouldn't be taking you to my favorite restaurant and I certainly wouldn't have mentioned my daughter."

My mouth goes dry, sweat breaking out across the small of my back at the same time. I shift my gaze away from him, blinking rapidly. He must sense my discomfort because he continues talking. "I don't know how other men treat you, but I would actually like to get to know you." He laughs then, a short, small huff. "Not that I haven't thought about you naked, let's just be clear there."

My eyes dart back to his, my breath hitching when I see the heat coming from them. "Well, that gives me something to aim for I guess." I grin sheepishly at him.

He snickers, followed by a long sigh. "You don't make it easy to say no, Gabby."

"So, just say yes?" I joke. "New NYPD motto?"

He leans forward, his voice growing deeper, my core tightening in response to the feral look he's giving me. "When I do say yes, I'll make sure it's worth the wait."

I drag my bottom lip between my teeth, and bite, needing something to distract me from the ache between my legs. One side of his mouth lifts in a sexy grin, his tongue sweeping across his own bottom lip as he leans back in his chair. *What a fucking tease, but holy crap, it's kind of nice having the tables turned on me for once.*

"I live in an apartment in Harlem, my wife left me for another man because I paid more attention to the job than her, I've been a detective for six years, I've got two older sisters, my father is white so I've got light eyes, and I think we covered the putting out part of the interrogation." He finishes by crunching into a chip, chewing loudly as he watches me.

"Does your daughter live with you?" No way am I letting him get the best of me.

"I get her every other weekend. If I have nights off, or want to take her any other time, my ex is great about it." He gets the waiter's attention and signals for another round of drinks. "They live really close to here actually."

My head tips to the side. "Here on the West Side?" It's a very wealthy part of town.

He scoffs. "Let's just say, she married up." New drinks are set in front of us, and he wastes no time lifting his for a sip. "You two would probably get along great."

"What's that supposed to mean?" My lips drawing together in a tight line. I don't care who you are, no one wants to be compared to the ex-wife.

His gaze snaps up to mine. "I just said the wrong thing, didn't I?" He drags a hand down his face. "I do that sometimes." He shakes his head once. "Shit. I'm sorry. I only meant that you both like nice things."

"Or maybe, we both just appreciate a man that pays attention to us." I snarl. "Not everything is about material things, Cameron."

"Shit, you're really pissed."

"No." I continue. "I just think that someone who is in your profession, wouldn't be so quick to judge a book by its cover. And in your attempt at *getting to know me better*, you'd dig a little deeper before assuming that all I care about is nice things."

He gets up then to slide in beside me on the bench I'm sitting on. His hand reaches up and cups my cheek, pulling my face to his until my eyes meet his. "I'm sorry. I say stupid things sometimes without thinking. She's not a bad person. She's a great mother and deserves every bit of happiness she has. I shouldn't compare you to her, because you're right. I don't know you well enough to judge or assume."

I stare back at him, my heart thumping erratically in response to his plea for my forgiveness, oddly endearing me to him even more. "Please don't do it again."

He nods "I won't."

He starts to push back, but I arch into the few inches separating us, my fingers bunching the soft material of his shirt against his chest to anchor him in place, then crush my mouth to his. His arm curls around my waist, fingers digging into the flesh of my back as he drags my body flush to his, my grip on his shirt releasing to slip around his neck. His tongue flicks against my lips before caressing them apart, mine snaking out to tangling with his, the taste of tequila and lime exploding across my buds. The hand cradling my face clenches, dipping my head back further, my leg sliding over his as I surge forward, a guttural moan catching in my throat.

I rock my aching core into his thigh, my knee bumping into his hard length, his hip jerking from the touch, my foot sliding down his calf, hitting something hard. I push away from him, panting, my head lowering to see what it is, then lift my gaze back to him in question.

He tightens his hold around my waist to shift me off of him but keeps me close, short bursts of air leaving his mouth before he speaks softly. "My gun."

My eyes fly wide. "You're wearing a gun?"

"Always." He states matter-of-factly.

"Is it loaded?" I ask quickly, placing my hand on his chest.

"Always." His brows furrow again. "Does that bother you?"

I press my fingers deeper as I lean into him. "It's fucking sexy as hell."

He chuckles, his chest vibrating under my touch. "I'm in so much trouble."

Before I can confirm his assessment, our server appears balancing a tray of steaming food. We dive in, the meal delicious, conversation flowing easily between us, as we get to know more about each other over standard date questions. We have one more drink after our meal, and then he motions for the waiter to bring our check.

CHAPTER Six

~Cameron~

We leave the restaurant after Graciela insists on packing up some food to take home with us, and, after twenty minutes of goodbyes. We walk hand in hand back to the car, engaging in another ten-minute make-out session against it, before I actually get her in it. We're almost back to her place, the raging hard-on throbbing between my legs making the ride feel longer than it really is.

She's got her hand on my thigh, literally inches from the danger zone, and I have no doubt that she knows it as she grazes her fingers slowly back and forth, a teasing smile on her lips. When I finally pull up in front of the hotel, I wonder how the hell I'm going to walk her inside. She turns to me and practically purrs out her next question. "Sure you don't want to come up?"

She has no idea how badly I want to take her up on her offer. But I like her, and I don't want this to just be about sex, so I decline, my dick pounding in frustration against the hard zipper of my jeans. "Not tonight Princess, but I'm off again tomorrow if you want to do something again?"

Her smile fades, her eyes fastening onto her hands in her lap. "I can't tomorrow."

"Oh, okay." I scratch my chin. "I've got to work the next three days after that, and then I'm off for four days, so just let me know."

"I work the weekend too, so sometime next week sounds great." She tilts her head and gives me a sexy smile. "Or there's always tonight? Our date doesn't have to end."

"You're relentless." I laugh, opening the door to step out of the car, pulling my jacket down in an attempt to hide my dick as I walk over to let her out.

I open her door, and she slips her hand into mine, pressing her body against me as she stands, shoving her middle against mine, as she stares up at me. "You're saying no, but at least one part of you is saying yes."

My head falls back as I let a groan of frustration fall free. "You're killing me."

"So come up." She mewls, peppering slow kisses over my chin before capturing my mouth. I grip the back of her head, plunging my tongue against hers, wanting to taste so much more of her.

I tear apart from her after a minute, stepping back. "Good night Gabby."

She shrugs, smiling, dropping a kiss to my cheek as she struts by. "Night handsome." She gives me a wave over her shoulder. "Sweet dreams."

I groan as I watch her body sway through the door being held open by the bellman, wanting nothing more than to follow her inside.

It's early Monday and I haven't been able to stop thinking about her. I'm sitting behind my desk at the precinct, working on some long, overdue paperwork, the bane of every detective's existence, completely distracted by thoughts of her. It's a little after three in the morning, and I know she's working at the hospital, so decide to text her.

~*Busy?*

She replies almost instantly, my heart leaping when her message pops up.

~*Bored. Quiet night. Trying to stay awake.*

I type quickly, hitting send before I change my mind.

~*Want some company?*

Her reply dings in less than four seconds.

~*Hell, yes!*

I type in one more quick message.

~*Coffee?*

I smile when I read her response.

~*Dating you may actually be better than sex. Extra cream, one sugar, please.*

I rise from my chair, stretching my arms over my head and yawn loudly. "I'm going to go make a coffee run. You want anything when I come back?"

Brian shifts his gaze from the game he's playing on his phone. "Want me to go with you?"

"Nah, I'm good." I stroll past him, snatching my wool trench off the coat rack as I pass by, leaving before he can protest. There's a McDonald's a couple of blocks from the precinct that I grab some coffees from, and then head to the hospital. I get there in less than ten minutes, three in the morning the ideal time to get anywhere quickly in this city, and park near the emergency room entrance.

I lift the tray off the seat, exit the car, and walk to the double doors. I'm about to press the call box to have her open the door when it swings open. She must be watching, and I smile, a feeling of satisfaction washing over me, knowing that she was waiting. She's standing on the other side of the doors, and even in scrubs with her hair pulled back in a ponytail, I'm stunned by her beauty.

"My hero." She places a hand over her heart as she tilts her chin up in mock adoration, rewarding me with a beautiful smile that almost bowls me over.

"At your service ma'am." I bow, holding the tray out to her. "We do aim to serve at the New York Police Department."

She hooks a finger under my chin, lifts it, and surprises me by pressing her lips against mine in a warm kiss. "Job well done, detective."

I tilt forward and capture her mouth for another quick kiss, then stand tall, lifting the tray a little higher. "I brought extras. I wasn't sure how many people might be working."

Her face lights up with a grin. "Cameron, that's the sweetest." She turns to walk into the triage room, shutting the door behind us. "Sit down if you want. I'll let the others know there's coffee."

"Okay." I place the tray on the counter, and pull each cup

of coffee out, separating the ones I ordered for us aside. A minute later, she's back, alone.

"Trey, he's the physician assistant on duty, is napping. Charlie and Sue said they'll come up in a few, they're changing some beds over."

I pick up the cup I brought for her and hold it out. "Extra cream, one sugar."

She takes it from me then steps between my legs, wrapping her hands loosely around my neck, the coffee warm against my shoulder. "Thanks." She bends her head to mine and kisses me lightly. "Did you miss me?"

I slide a hand to her hip and twist her, pushing her down onto my lap. I grab the coffee from her with my other hand to put it on the counter next to us. "Let's just say I've taken a few cold showers since last Thursday." I skim my hand up her back, wrap my fingers around the back of her neck to pull her to me, claiming her lips with a need I hadn't realized could exist. Her mouth opens, and I dip my tongue inside, stroking against hers, the heat of her breath becoming one with mine.

She shifts her body, lacing her arms around me, hugging her chest to mine, a whimper escaping when I cup her breast over her shirt and squeeze. Her head falls back, and I graze kisses in a wet path down her long neck, then drag my tongue up capturing the trail, before crushing my mouth back against hers. My cock pulses as it hardens against the material of my slacks, pressing against her stomach. My fingers dig into the soft flesh of her hip as I tug her into my dick, thrusting myself forward as I do, grinding against her.

Her mouth parts from mine on a small gasp, her eyes wide as they drop to my waist, her tongue darting out to swipe against her lower lip. *Jesus what I wouldn't do to have those lips around me right now.* She releases a hand from my neck and drops it on top of the bulge between us, her fingers tightening around my length as she lifts her eyes to mine. "Another concealed weapon?" Her shoulders start to shake a second before her hand slaps over her mouth in an attempt to quelch the laughter spilling out of her. It takes less than five seconds for me to recover from the surprise of her question, my own laughter matching hers.

"What's so funny?"

My head snaps toward the sound of the new voice in the room, Gabby jumping off my lap to stand in front of me. "Nothing." She waves her hand dismissively in the air. "Inside joke." She moves toward the counter. "Want a coffee?"

He scratches at the scruff on his chin, tired eyes looking back and forth at us, then takes one of the cups from Gabby. I stand, thankful my trench is still on because it's covering my hard-on, and extend my hand, "I'm Cameron, Gabby's friend."

His brows lift. "Ah, the cop." He grips my hand with his and pumps it once. "Nice to meet you, I'm Trey." He tosses a glance at Gabby. "I feel like I already know you after listening to this one go on and on about you to Charlotte."

Gabby's face flushes red, her eyes bulging wide as her fist flies out to punch Trey in the arm. "Shut the hell up, asshole!"

"Uh-oh, what'd you do babe?" A petite, brunette walks into the room, her round belly leading the way, her eyes crinkled up in a smile.

"Nothing!" He rubs his arm where Gabby hit him,

shooting her a nasty glance. "I was just telling Cameron," He pauses, nodding in my direction, "how I feel like I already know him after listening to you two gossip the other day."

"Trey!" One hand stops rubbing the side of her belly and lands on her hip in a fist. "You're lucky all she did was punch you." She rolls her eyes dramatically, then shifts her attention to me. "So, you're the cop?"

"Yep." I chuckle, my hand skimming over my head as I nod. "But why do I have the feeling I'm the one about to be interrogated?"

She smirks. "Nonsense." She pulls a pad and a pen out of her scrub pocket and hands it to me, winking. "But if you could just jot down your full name, date of birth, and social security number on here, that'd be great."

Gabby yanks the pad from her hand and slams it on the counter. "Okay, okay, you've both had your fun." She shakes her head then looks at me. "That's Charlie, by the way; she's *supposed* to be my best friend. She's engaged to Trey, now that she's all knocked up and everything."

Charlie sticks her tongue out at Gabby, then offers me a sweet smile. "Seriously, nice to meet you, Cameron."

"You too Charlie." My phone rings from the pocket of my coat, so I excuse myself for a minute. I realize as soon as I see Brian's name on the caller-id that I've been gone much longer than I intended. I hit answer and bring the phone to my ear. "Justice."

"Where the fuck did you go?"

"On my way back now." I fire back, not feeling the need to explain myself.

"Someone just called in another beaten prostitute. She's at Lenox Hill."

"Shit." I mutter. "This is the fourth one in two weeks."

"Yep."

"I'll text you when I'm out front. Ten minutes." I don't bother with a good-bye and just end the call. I spin around to Gabby and frown. "Sorry, duty calls. I have to go." I toss a wave at Trey and Charlie. "Nice to meet you both."

They both return the sentiment, each giving me a wave back.

"Is everything okay?" Gabby walks next to me as I leave the triage room.

"Another beaten woman, same MO as the one we brought here last week." I grimace, turning to her as we stop short of the exit. "She's the fourth one in two weeks."

"Shit. That's scary." Her brows furrow. "Is there a connection?"

"Other than them all being prostitutes, not that we've found yet."

"They're all prostitutes?" Her body stiffens under my touch.

A frustrated sigh leaves me. "I'm sorry, I really have to go. Brian's waiting for me." I rest my forehead against hers, closing my eyes as I press my lips to hers, enjoying the last moments of pleasure I'll probably have for the next several hours. "I'll call you later."

"Okay." She stutters out, her fingers dropping from mine as I race out the door.

CHAPTER SEVEN

~Gabrielle~

"So, you really like him?" Charlie takes a bite out of the breakfast burrito I delivered to her fifteen minutes ago. It's a couple of hours before our next shift at the hospital, so technically we should be eating dinner right now. We start at seven in the evening and work a twelve-hour shift. We're required to work two weeks of night shifts every eight weeks at the hospital, and we're starting our second week tonight. The nice thing, is that we usually only have to work three days in a row. Because of the night differential, and the overtime after eight hours, we easily earn the equivalent, if not more, than what we would have if we worked forty physical hours. Unfortunately, it's spring break week, and we're short staffed because many of the nurses and doctors take vacation during this time, so we're both pulling an extra shift tonight.

"I mean, yeah, I think so." I fidget with the cup in my hand.

"The guy delivered coffee to you in the middle of the night." She waves her fork at me. "He helped a beaten girl he found while he was out jogging. And, he's gorgeous." She shoves my arm. "What do you mean, you think so?"

"Did I tell you about his gun?" I arch a brow, looking over at her. "He carries it with him even when he's not on duty." I let out a longing sigh. "I mean, that's fucking sexy."

"And yet you haven't slept with him?" She giggles sarcastically.

"Not because I don't want to." I throw my hands up. "I mean, you saw him. He's all kinds of hot. I want to climb him like a tree. He keeps shutting me down."

I whip my head in Charlie's direction when she starts laughing. "Oh poor, little sexually deprived Gabby. Someone is actually making you wait to have sex."

"Shut up, bitch." I pick up a salsa packet and toss it playfully at her. "We've only been out once."

"Isn't that all it usually takes with you?" She smirks, winking at me.

"Very funny." I pluck a fried potato off her plate and pop it in my mouth.

"Does he know about your job at Temptations?"

I stop chewing and stare back at her for a minute before answering. "No."

"Are you going to tell him?"

I look away, drumming my fingernails against the countertop before I answer. "I mean until it becomes something more, do I really need to? I haven't even heard from him since he brought us coffee."

She scoffs. "Gabby, that was fourteen hours ago. It's obvious he likes you. You need to think about what you're going to do if you want to keep seeing him."

I groan and drop my head into my arms, mumbling in protest. "I don't know how to do this." I lift my head to look her in the eye. "You know me. I've always lived by the catch and release rule, and that's been working just fine for me."

"You deserve more Gabby." She reaches out to place her warm hand over mine. "It doesn't have to be a bad thing to want something more."

"Yeah, until my heart gets stomped on. My way means no muss, no fuss."

"It's also a pretty lonely way to live Gabs. Is that really what you want?"

"Ugh!" I slide my hand out from hers to cover my face. "I don't know what I want, that's the problem."

"You will." She leans over and gives me a hug. "When you know, you know and when you do, the decision will be easy. Trust me."

I wrap my arms around her, returning the affection she's giving me. "Love you, friend."

"Love you more."

"Have I been replaced?" Trey jokes from behind us.

We break apart, giggling, Charlie padding over to him. "Never, baby." She stretches up on her toes to give him a kiss on the lips. "Did you get enough sleep?"

"Yeah." He brushes a hand through his hair, tousling it. "I'll be glad when these damn night shifts are over though. They're killing me."

She lays a hand on her belly to rub the large bump. "This little girl kicks so much now that I barely sleep anyway."

Trey drops to his knees, grasping her belly between his hands, and starts talking to the bump. "Be gentle on Momma, little one." I smile when he peppers kisses over her stomach, then stands back up, pulling Charlie into his arms to press a kiss to her mouth. I still can't believe they're having a baby, even though the evidence is protruding from her waistline. A year ago we were out dancing until dawn, babies the furthest thing from our minds. I guess it doesn't take long for some things to change.

"Okay you love birds, are you going to get dressed and come to work with me, or should I leave you alone?" I tease, genuinely happy that my best friend has found so much contentment.

Almost fourteen hours later, after the busiest night shift, I can remember in months, I've never been so relieved to leave the hospital. The only saving grace is that I didn't have a chance after midnight to check my phone to see if Cameron texted me. Trey took Charlie home a few minutes ago, anxious to get her off her feet and in bed for some rest. I scowl when I step outside and realize it's raining, and am about to turn back inside when I see him. He's standing under an umbrella, on the far side of the parking lot, a wide smile lifting his lips when he realizes I see him.

I feel my cheeks rise, a weightlessness settling over me, unnerving me slightly when I realize this might be joy I'm feeling. Before I can overthink it, he strides toward me, all thoughts vanishing, when he sweeps me into an embrace to crush his mouth to mine. I fling my arms around his neck, pressing my body flush to his, and melt into his kiss. After a moment, we tear apart, the raindrops splattering around us as I beam at him. "What are you doing here?"

"Would you believe me if I told you I was in the neighborhood?" He's still holding me in his arms, and it feels better than I want to admit to myself.

I flash my teeth in a quick smile. "It's a bit cliché, but honestly, I'm really happy to see you, whatever the reason."

"I thought I'd take you to breakfast." He pecks another kiss to my lips. "If you're not too tired."

"I'm suddenly wide awake."

"Come on then." He turns, leaving his arm wrapped around my waist. "Your chariot awaits." He leads me to his car, opening the passenger door, holding the umbrella over me until I'm settled.

He jogs around the front of the car, closes the umbrella, then climbs in behind the wheel to start the car. I put my seatbelt on without prompting this time, earning a satisfied nod from him. "I'm sorry I haven't been able to call or text." He slides into traffic. "I ended up working until yesterday afternoon, and passed out as soon as my head hit the pillow when I got home."

"I honestly didn't even notice." I lie. "Work was crazy busy for me too."

He turns his attention away from the road to gaze at me for what seems like an eternity, making me feel like he can see right through me before he finally responds. "Jesus, you're tough."

My brows shoot up. "What do you mean?"

He shakes his head once. "Not going to let down that wall easily, are you?" His knuckles tighten around the steering wheel. "It's okay if you missed me Gabby. It doesn't have to mean any more than that. I sure as shit missed you."

"We barely even know each other Cameron." I squeeze my hands into tight fists on my lap. "We had one date and you brought me coffee. I don't think you really know me well enough to miss me yet."

He yanks the car over to the side of the road, throws it into park, then turns to look at me, his eyes blazing. "Your hair smells like coconut. You don't wear any makeup when you work, which I think makes you look even more beautiful. Every time I hold your hand, I feel your pulse quicken beneath the pad of my thumb. Your eyes change color depending upon your mood. They're more gray right now, which means you're nervous. You clench your hands into fists when you're not sure if you should be angry or scared."

I look down at my hands, flinching when I notice them and spread my fingers wide on my thighs.

"You like tequila, not because it's cool, but because you actually like the flavor of it. You aren't afraid to dress like a woman, but feel just as comfortable in sneakers and scrubs. When you laugh really hard, you always cover your mouth with your hand. You want everyone to believe you're happy living all alone in a fancy hotel, but the real reason you stay there is so that you're always surrounded by people, because I think, you're actually really lonely."

My chest tightens, making it difficult to draw a breath, let alone speak, my mouth suddenly dry as sand. I know he's a detective, and therefore, more likely to notice all the small details about a person that another might not, but these things are more than details. I think he might actually know me better than friends who have known me for years. I turn my head to look at him, my eyes narrowed in confusion, my thoughts spinning like a tornado. I open my mouth to speak, but I only blink, close my mouth, then open it again. "I actually really hate wearing scrubs."

His head falls back as he erupts in laughter. He turns to me, shaking his head. "That's what you took away from that?"

"I just--" I let out a short growl. "Fine, I missed you a little too."

He responds by chuckling, then slides his fingers through mine to pull my hand onto his lap.

"Where are you taking me for breakfast?" Definitely, time to change the subject.

"Have you been to the Grey Dog before? It's in the village." He pulls the car back into traffic to continue our journey.

I shake my head as I answer, "I don't think so."

"It's the best. You'll love it."

He's right. Thirty minutes later, we're both digging into our food, barely speaking because it's so good. By the time we finish and Cameron pays the bill, the rain has stopped. Now that I'm full of food, and have sat still for a bit, exhaustion sets in. When we're back in the car, I ask if he minds taking me home, letting him know I'm beat. The ride back to my place is quiet, but not uncomfortable, and as we drive, I absorb the sights of the city coming to life for the day, through heavy eyelids.

"Hey, sleeping beauty." I blink, Cameron coming into focus, kneeling beside me. "You fell asleep."

"Oh my god, I'm so sorry." I groan, placing a hand over my mouth as it turns into a yawn. "Are you sure I just can't stay here?"

"Come on." He reaches over to unbuckle me, then pulls me gently from the car. "Let's get you to bed."

I cock one side of my mouth up in a half-hearted attempt at a sexy smile. "Are you coming with me?"

Chuckling, he wraps an arm around my waist as he guides me to the entrance of the hotel. "I think you need to get some rest."

"Awe, come on. Just come up and tuck me in." I turn my head to plant a kiss on his neck to try and tempt him.

"How about we do something later? You're off the next couple days, right?"

"Yes, the next three nights."

"So, why don't I pick you up later?"

We've entered the hotel and are standing just inside the doors. "Why don't you come here instead, for dinner? Around eight? Want to do that?"

He looks at me for a moment, then finally nods. "Okay. Sounds good."

"Good." I step into him to capture his mouth with mine, clenching his jacket in my hands to pull him close to me. We break apart after a minute, both of us flushed. I press the button for the elevator and step in when the doors open. He waits for me to press the button for my floor, and starts to turn away. As the doors slide shut, I call out to him, "Cameron, don't forget to bring your weapon." Then flash him a naughty smile as I wave.

CHAPTER
Eight

~Cameron~

Today has been the longest fucking day ever. I take a deep breath as the elevator rises to the twelfth floor towards Gabby's apartment to try and calm my nerves. I went on an eight-mile run earlier, picked Willow up after school, took her for ice cream, stopped at Macy's to pick up some new boxers, (because hey, underwear matters, even to a guy), and finally, took a long, cold shower. All in an attempt to expend some of the energy that's been coursing through my veins in anticipation of tonight.

I could tell her no. Hell, I'd been doing that for over a week, but if I was being honest with myself, I was tired of waiting. I wanted her just as much as she wanted me. My cock twitches every single damn time I think about her, but knowing I was going to see her today, made every thought about her more unbearable than usual. I'm hoping I can make it through dinner instead of throwing her on the first surface I see. The elevator slows to a stop, the doors sliding open with a whoosh, my heart knocking against my chest as I step out.

I twist my head, investigating the hallway, and notice there are only two doors on the whole floor, 12L, and 12R. Her residence takes up half the god damn floor of the hotel. Holy shit, this is a whole new level of rich. I stride to the door labeled 12R, take a fortifying breath, and knock on the door. It swings open less than five seconds later, the breath I just took, caught in my throat as I stare at the woman standing in front of me.

"Hi." Her head tilts, a sexy smile crooking up one side of her mouth in the same direction. "Come in."

She's wearing a blue velvet wrap dress, her eyes reflecting the rich color, sparkling as she gazes at me, her bottom lip caught between her teeth. I'm not sure which is deeper, the V dipping between her cleavage, or the slit exposing most of her left thigh. The dress is secured by a single tie at her waist, calling to me like a siren to pull it loose.

I take two large strides to her, closing the distance between us, slamming the door behind me as I do, and smash my mouth on hers. My hands are in her hair, fisting the locks as I crush her to me, a guttural moan sounding as her fingers dig into my shoulders. I push her backwards with the force of my body until she bumps up against the wall, an oomph escaping around her lips as my cock grinds against her center.

I drag one hand down her curves until I find the tie, and I tug, my lips devouring hers, the dress falling open. She's completely naked underneath, and my dick throbs against my jeans as it hardens completely. I stroke my fingers over her nipple, plucking the peak into a tight bud, her mouth gaping against mine with a moan. I nip at her lip, her chin, her neck, and finally her breast as I work the belt on my pants with one hand.

She pushes my hand aside, unbuckling the metal before tearing the button of my jeans open. I feel her palm on my ass as she shoves my pants down, then drags back around my waist to wrap around my cock.

"Fuck." I hiss out, releasing her nipple, fusing my mouth back over hers, my fingers digging into her ass as I lift her to line my cock up against her center, then surge forward, driving my cock into her in one plunge.

We both cry out, our bodies frozen for a moment in time at the connection, her nails biting into the flesh of my ass, my head falling back in bliss. I rock forward, her legs locking around me as her mouth finds mine again, my hips moving to piston in and out of her, faster and faster. Her back slams against the wall each time I drive into her, her nails tearing at my skin as she clings onto me, both of us grunting in pleasure. Raw, unfiltered need consumes both of us as I fuck her, my cock sinking into her again and again until I feel her muscles tighten around me, my name leaving her lips on a scream. I shove myself into her as deep as I can, her walls clenching onto my dick, and then I push even deeper, my balls tightening as my cock swells inside of her. I yank myself out, exploding against her hip as I do, my release jerking out in spurts against her.

Our breaths are leaving us in short pants as our foreheads rest together, my eyes locking onto hers when I blink them open. One side of my mouth quirks up. "Hi."

"Hi." She lets out a low chuckle. "Well, that was easier than I thought it was going to be."

I chuckle back. "I really was going to try and wait until after dinner, but damn woman, in that dress you made it impossible."

She tilts her head forward to nip at my lips. "Then my plan worked."

I capture her mouth and push my chest into hers, not wanting the connection between us to end. I finish the kiss then whisper against her mouth. "You're so fucking beautiful, Gabby."

Her head slides into the crook of my neck as her grip on me tightens. She holds onto me for several long seconds before she releases me to push against my body. "Let's go clean up." I take a step back to glance down at the sticky mess clinging to both of us and nod. "Come on, the bathroom is this way." I follow behind as she leads the way.

There's a bathroom, just off the foyer, that she points to. "You can use that one." She points to the right. "I'll go clean up in my room."

"Okay." I watch her dress swing over the curve of her ass as she walks away, and I enter the bathroom. Shit, that didn't quite go like I was expecting. I knew we were most likely going to have sex tonight, but I sure wasn't planning on fucking her up against the first wall we came to. I stare at my reflection in the mirror and shake my head. "Now what?"

It's more than obvious that Gabby is the kind of woman that likes to have sex, and if I had to guess, she plays the field, not one to take anything too seriously. I didn't want to be one of those guys with her. I liked her. I felt a connection with her that I couldn't explain, and one I hadn't felt with anyone before. Not even my ex-wife. I blow out a long breath as I realize I'm the one that's going to be fucked if she doesn't feel the same.

I wash my hands, rinse my face, then clean things up below my waist, buckling myself back up when I'm done. When I step out of the bathroom, she's leaning against the opposite wall, waiting for me. My dick actually twitches at the sight of her. She's wearing a black cotton dress, with thin shoulder straps holding up a fitted top that flares into a short skirt. It's simple, but like everything else, she makes it look elegant.

"You changed." I let my eyes trail down her frame, pausing briefly on her chest, her nipples protruding from the thin fabric.

"Had to." She pushes herself off the wall to lean her body into mine as she looks up at me. "You Monica Lewinsky'd mine."

I bend my head forward to brush a kiss against her lips. "I'd apologize, but I'm not really sorry."

"Neither am I." She smiles sexily back at me.

"I would have put a condom on, but it all happened so fast." I explain, wanting her to know I'm not the kind of guy who goes around sticking my cock in everyone.

"I've got an IUD." Her brows furrow. "Do I need to be worried?"

"Do I?" I counter.

"I get checked regularly."

"My ex is the only other woman I've ever-"

"You've only had sex with one other woman?" She blurts, eyes popping wide as she shoves back from me.

"-had sex with, without a condom on." I finish, then grab her hand to yank her back against me. "Did it seem like I didn't know what I was doing because I'd be more than happy to try again if that's the impression I left."

"Oooh, I think I like it when I make you a little mad." She teases, pressing her mouth against mine. "Did you bring your handcuffs and your gun, detective? You wanna arrest me for false accusations?"

"If I didn't think you'd like it so much, I might actually consider it." I swat her on the ass, eliciting a low growl and a hip thrust into my groin, my brow arching in surprise at her reaction. "I see that's not going to work either."

"I guess it depends on what purpose you want the punishment to serve." She purrs back, a low ache starting to throb below my waist.

"I thought you were going to feed me?" I place my hands on her upper arms to gently pry her off my body.

"Oh Cameron, so many ways I could quench your hunger if you'd like." She takes a bold step toward me and drags her fingers down my chest, hooking her fingers into my belt when she reaches my waist.

I place my hands over hers to stop her from unbuckling my belt. As much as I love the direction this is going on, I don't want her to think that this is all I came for. "Later." I tug her up my body to sweep my mouth against hers. "Show me your apartment."

She blinks back at me, I think surprised that I'm not already ramming my dick down her throat, then nods. "Okay, sure." She takes my hand and leads me room by room through the apartment. There are three different bedrooms, all off the hallway we're standing in, so she shows me those first. Her bedroom is the largest, with long windows that overlook the park on the far side wall. The room is decorated in dark pink, and she has white fur accents throughout. Very feminine indeed.

The living room and dining room are both large and decorated tastefully with cushioned sofas in muted colors. There are a few family photos that I glance at as we walk through, but in general, the rooms are fairly sparse. The thing I notice, only because it's in contrast to everything else in the apartment, is the huge aquarium between the two-floor length windows facing the park. It's filled with colorful, tropical fish, the bubbling of the filter echoing a soothing rhythm of sound throughout the large space. I point to it. "Nice fish tank."

"I love fish." She strides over to it, brushing her fingers over the glass. "Especially the really colorful ones. They're so pretty and it's so peaceful to look at."

I drop a kiss on top of her head. "You're full of surprises."

She shrugs, then pulls me toward the kitchen, which is completely clean, without a trace of any cooking or food present.

"What exactly were your plans for dinner?" I wonder out loud.

"Room service, of course." She states like it should be so obvious. "You didn't think I was going to cook, did you?"

I laugh deeply. "I did actually."

"Oh no." She shakes a finger at me. "I don't do that."

"What?" I chuckle again. "Cook?"

"Yeah." She nods. "I burn water."

"Well, at least you look pretty standing in here." I back her into the counter to press a kiss against her lips. "And lucky for you, I can cook."

"Yeah, but I don't have anything for you to cook, so tonight you're getting whatever you like from the room service menu." She shrugs, unapologetically.

"Room service it is." I finally concede, kissing her one more time before letting her go. She takes the menu out a drawer, and after we both decide what we want, she calls to place the order with the kitchen.

"You want to see if we can find something to watch on television?" She suggests, leaving the kitchen as she heads toward the living room.

"Sure."

She grabs the remote out of a drawer in a side table, then plops down in the middle of one of the puffy couches. She pats the spot beside her inviting me to sit, which I do, one arm sliding behind her on the back of the couch, as she turns on the T.V. "What's your favorite movie?"

I think for a minute. "Training Day."

She frowns. "Haven't seen it."

"You haven't seen it?" My mouth falling open in shock. "Denzel Washington. Ethan Hawke. It's like the best cop movie ever."

"Well, there you go then." She shrugs. "Not my kind of movie."

"Okay, tell me yours. I can hardly wait."

"No." She purses her lips. "I'm not going to tell you. You're just going to make fun of me and tell me what a typical girl I am, so I'm not even going there."

"Please don't tell me it's Pretty Woman." I tease, knowing I hit the mark when her eyes go wide and she snaps her head away from me. "It is! I knew it!"

"Pretty Woman is a modern-day fairy tale of love. I don't know why you think it's funny that I like that movie." She crosses her arms and glares at me.

"It's so unrealistic! I mean, come on, do you really think he's going to live happily ever after with a prostitute? When it really sinks in how many men she's slept with?"

Her eyes narrow as she stares at me for a long, hard minute before finally responding. "Who cares how many men she slept with. You think that defines who she is?"

"Um, yeah. She's a hooker. So, I'd say yes. And I deal with them every single day in my line of work, so I have a first-row seat to what these women are like. There ain't no Julia Roberts in the mix."

"So, what if I told you I've slept with a bunch of guys. Does that make my worth, less to you?"

"Listen, I know you aren't a virgin by any means Gabby, but there's a big difference between sleeping with some guys, and taking money from them to do it. The movie sets up unrealistic expectations for girls. I know I'm not ever going to let my daughter watch it."

Her nostrils flare as she lifts her chin and begins to speak. "Cameron, I should probably tell you that-" The doorbell rings, followed by, "room service" shouted from the other side of the door, interrupting her. She shakes her head as she stands. "I'll get that."

I rise off the couch. "Let me help."

"No." She snaps at me, then exhales loudly. "Please, I've got this."

My brows arch high, and I step back. "Okay." I literally may have just been saved by the bell because I think she was getting ready to ask me to leave. *Fuck. What a dick I am. Next time just tell her you like the movie and shut up.*

She's back in less than a minute, followed by a sharp-dressed waiter pushing a cart. "Where would you like me to set up, Ms. Reed?"

She looks at me. "Do you want to eat at the table, or in here?"

I think we better stay the hell away from the television. "How about the dining room?"

"Fine." She turns to the waiter and motions him toward the dining room. *Shit.* Nothing is ever fine when a woman says fine. I walk up behind her, slide a hand around her waist, then pull her back against my front. I nuzzle my nose against her neck, inhaling her scent, as I drop a kiss above her ear. "I'm sorry." I whisper. "I didn't mean to make you upset."

Her body relaxes as she exhales, her hand covering mine as she does. "I'm not mad."

The waiter turns to us. "All set, Ms. Reed. Have a nice dinner." He leaves the room, taking the cart with him, the door shutting behind him confirming his exit.

I spin her around to hold her face in my hands. "Whatever I said to upset you, I'm sorry."

She blinks and lifts the corners of her mouth into a tiny smile. "It's nothing. It's just a stupid movie. Let's eat."

CHAPTER
Nine

~Gabrielle~

We sit at the dining room table, me in front of the salad I ordered, and him in front of his burger. I was seconds away from telling him about my job at Temptations when the waiter knocked, and now I'm not sure if I should say anything or not. He just made it very clear how he feels about prostitutes. Technically, I'm not a prostitute. I'm an escort. And I've never once asked someone for money when I've had sex, but it doesn't mean it wasn't left behind for me. I've donated anything left for me to the church down the street. I only started working at Temptations because sleeping with rich, sophisticated men was a lot nicer than sleeping with the douche bags picking me up in bars.

Shit, shit, shit! See? This is why I've always subscribed to the catch and release program. This is what happens when you like someone. And, I like him. I don't want him to get the wrong idea about me if I do tell him. Besides, who knows if this is even going to go anywhere. Most guys split after the third date, so I'll just wait to see what happens. When I'm finally done convincing myself that I've made the right decision, I smile in Cameron's direction. "How's your burger?"

He finishes the bite he's chewing and nods. "It's perfect. How's the salad?"

"Good." *Great, we've resorted to small talk.* "Oh, do you want some wine? I actually do have some of that in my fridge."

"Sure, I'll have a glass."

I go to the kitchen to pull one of the bottles of white out of the refrigerator, grab the opener out of the drawer and bring them to the table. "Got to grab glasses." I go back into the kitchen, smiling when I hear the pop of the cork, happy he opened it for us. I suck at trying to get the damn cork out of the bottle. I carry the glasses to the dining room and set them on the table in front of him. He pours us each some wine as I sit back down. He uses the tips of his fingers to slide my glass closer to me, and I take it, bringing it to my lips for a much-needed drink. "What do you want to do after we eat?"

"I definitely do not want to watch a movie." He smirks, and I giggle in response, some of the tension finally breaking between us.

"They usually have someone playing the piano down in the bar during the week, and sometimes they have jazz on Wednesdays." I suggest.

"Honestly, I'd rather just stay here with you." He glances

over his shoulder into the living room. "Maybe we could just light a fire, drink some wine and talk?"

"Or, you know, make-out." I flirt back at him, taking another sip of my wine.

He cracks a smile while shaking his head. "Yeah, maybe that too."

We finish dinner, place the dishes into the sink, and then move into the living room. I flick the switch to turn the gas fireplace on, while Cameron pours us each some more of the wine. I snuggle into one corner of the couch, and Cameron sits about a foot from me, turned sideways, leaning into the back cushions. I put my feet in his lap and wiggle my toes. "Hope you don't have a thing against feet."

He wraps his hand around the top of my foot, massaging my toes. "Nope and yours are pretty sexy."

"Oh, that reminds me." I sit up a little taller. "Alexa, play my sexy playlist." A second later, music starts streaming softly through the living room.

"You have a sexy playlist?" He tries to hide a smile as he takes a sip of his wine.

"Doesn't everyone?" I shrug.

"Well, that's the first time I've seen anyone use an Alexa, so that's kind of cool."

"She's my best friend. Keeps me company." I take a sip of my wine, a little embarrassed that I just admitted a digital voice is sometimes my only companion.

"Tell me something about you that no one else knows." He challenges, his fingers digging into the arch of my foot, causing me to squirm in delight.

"Oh God, I have to think about this one." I tap a finger

against my forehead as I search through my memories, then look over at him. "I never went to prom."

"Is that a big secret?" He frowns. "I was looking for something a little deeper here."

I hold my finger up. "It's the reason I never went to prom that's a secret. Because of course, I was asked. A couple of times actually."

He scoots a little closer, his eyes glued to mine. "Okay, now I'm interested."

"I couldn't dance." I reveal, slapping a hand over my face. "And I was too embarrassed to ask or tell anyone, so I just didn't go."

"Wait, you missed one of a girl's biggest rites of passage in high school because you couldn't dance?"

I nod up and down, my lips smashed into a straight line of embarrassment. "I was supposed to be one of the cool kids. How would it look if I had to ask someone else how to dance?"

"But no one thought it was weird that you didn't go to the prom?"

"I made up some lie about having to go to an Aunt's funeral or something."

"So, did you ever learn to dance?"

I watch his fingers graze lazily over my calf, then glance up at him. "I did. When I turned eighteen, the summer before I went to college, I hired a dance instructor and took private lessons."

"Show me." He slides my feet off his lap, then rises, reaching over to pull me up next to him. He takes my glass out of my hand and sets both of them on the table in front of the couch.

"Right now?"

"Right now."

I tilt my head and let out a nervous laugh. "Okay." I step into his arms, one hand falling into his, the other wrapping around his shoulder. "Alexa, turn the music up." Thinking Out Loud by Ed Sheeran fills the room, and Cameron starts swaying with me to the rhythm. One foot sweeps between his as he turns me, his hand planted firm and wide between my exposed shoulder blades, the heat radiating from his palm through my skin. His cheek is pressed against mine, his lips moving near my ear as he sings the words to the song softly, my body melting into his with each rotation.

My hand bunches the material under it, my lips parting as I draw in a slow breath, my heart stuttering to a beat all its own, as he draws me closer, my waist pressed firmly against his hard length. We spin in another slow circle, my head slightly dizzy from the motion, so I close my eyes, tightening my fingers locked around his. The song ends, and Cameron stills the motion of our bodies, my eyes fluttering open as his cheek leaves mine. "You can dance." He says softly.

"And you can sing." I breathe out.

"Eh." He lifts one shoulder. "Not really." He releases me as he takes a small step back.

My eyes drop, locking onto the bulge below his waist, his hand moving over it in an attempt to hide it. I reach out, taking his hand into mine, then turn, pulling him with me. "Come." He follows without a word as I lead him into my bedroom, releasing him when we're standing at the foot of my bed. I keep walking until I get to the wall, and press a button that closes the drapes to shut the city outside away from us. I spin around to face him, his eyes glued to me, as I prowl back to him, stopping when I'm six inches away. "Can I take your shirt off?"

His tongue darts out to sweeps along his bottom lip as he nods, his gaze never leaving mine. "Yes."

I lift my fingers to the top button of his shirt, work to unfasten it and then move to the next, repeating the action until his shirt lays open. I skim down his smooth skin, my fingers tracing the ridges of muscle defining his abdomen. He giggles, his hand locking my wrist, lifting it off his stomach.

"You're ticklish." I grin at him.

"Now you know one of my secrets."

I want to know them all, but I'll start with seeing the rest of him naked. Because holy hell, so far, he's pretty fucking amazing. "Take your pants off."

"Demanding thing, aren't you?" He moves to release his belt, and I pull my lip between my teeth as he toes off his shoes, then pushes his pants down. My eyes pop wide when he pulls them off and I see the gun strapped to his ankle. He's bent over but glances up at me as he removes the holster, then stands up straight. "This doesn't scare you?"

"Why would it scare me?" I frown. "You're not going to use it on me, are you?"

He moves to my dresser to place the gun on its surface, returning to stand in front of me in just a tight pair of boxers, his length hard and jutting under the material. "Not the weapon I planned on using on you."

"Music to my ears." I hook a finger under each strap of my dress to drag them over my shoulders. I pull lower, exposing my breasts, then my stomach, and then finally, let go, the dress sliding completely off me, leaving me naked. I step out of the fabric pooled at my feet, place my hands on his chest and shove him onto the bed, falling to my knees in front of him. I spread his legs, shifting my body between them, my hand skimming up his thigh until my fingers wrap around his length.

I lift my gaze until it locks with his, then I bend to drag my mouth over the material trapping his cock, the outline bursting against the smooth silk of his boxers. His head falls back against his shoulders on a groan, as I squeeze his shaft, his hips jutting up. I slide his boxers off his waist, capturing his cock in my mouth as it bounces free, sucking him deep, his fingers latching onto my hair as I swallow him. I loosen the suction I have around his length to swirl my tongue around the head of his cock, then suck him deep again. He thrusts, driving himself halfway down my throat causing me to gag, my hands gripping onto his hips to push him back as I lift off of him.

His grasp on my scalp tightens to haul me up over his body, his hand moving to the base of my neck as he claims my mouth in a brutal kiss, our teeth clacking together as he sweeps his tongue against mine. I straddle his waist to lower my pussy against his hard length, sliding my hips forward, my juices coating him. I reach my hand between us to guide him inside me, but he bucks away from me, the force of his action rolling me onto my back, his body looming over me now.

"Not yet." He growls, right before his lips claim mine, nipping them gently before sliding down my body. He strokes his tongue over my nipple, causing it to harden into a tight point, then switches to my other breast, laving it to attention as well. He sucks each tip into his mouth, one at a time, his hands cupping my breasts together tightly, his cock weeping against the inside of my thigh. My fingers clench onto his bare scalp, as I pant out my approval, my back arching up with each pull of his mouth.

He releases my breasts and drags his tongue down my stomach, spinning it around my belly button, then lower, his torso between my legs now. His hands slide up the inside of my thighs as he spreads my legs wide, the heat of his mouth against my center as he flicks his tongue over my clit. I clutch the comforter like an anchor to try and keep my hips still as he flicks again, before latching his mouth over my sensitive bud sucking it hard. I yell out his name, my fists clenching wildly when he slides a finger into my wet channel and begins pumping slowly in and out of me as he laps against my clit.

I thrash my head back and forth, my eyes scrunched tight as I feel my orgasm building, the muscles in my pussy starting to quiver around the two fingers he has in me now. "I'm going to cum." I pant out.

He draws his fingers slowly out of me, laps at me one final time, then rises back up over my body. He grabs his cock in one hand and guides it to my center, letting go as the tip enters me, his hips rocking forward, his entire length sinking into me. He rears back, then surges into me again in short, steady strokes that drag against my clit, my hands digging into his ass, urging him to thrust deeper.

I grind my hips into his, meeting him thrust for thrust, sweat coating our bodies as we rub together. "Harder Cameron, harder." I beg, a tingling sensation zapping up my toes, through my legs, straight to my pussy as it begins to convulse around his cock, my body shuddering under him as I orgasm, my mouth open in a silent scream. Five strokes later I feel his body tighten against mine as he buries himself deep one final time, his release exploding, coating my insides in hot spurts, my name tumbling from his lips on a groan as he collapses over me.

Hours later, sunlight streaming through the cracks in the drapes, I drag my eyes open and roll over, my body colliding against Cameron, still asleep, gloriously laid out before me. My hand flies to my mouth, which is turned up in a surprised smile, as realization dawns that he didn't leave. I'm not alone in my bed. He stayed. There was no money laying somewhere instead, in his place. I knew right then and there that it was time for me to leave Temptations.

CHAPTER Ten

~Cameron~

Hot, wet kisses trailing up my shoulder have me turning my head as my eyes flutter open. I glance down, her long, dark tresses, soft as silk, sliding up my chest as her lips skim my neck, over my chin, then finally latch onto mine, claiming them in a gentle kiss. "Good morning handsome."

"Waking up to you in my arms just made it the best morning ever." I tilt my head forward to capture her mouth with mine.

"You stayed." She sits up beside me, crossing her legs Indian style, her warm hand resting over my heart.

"Why would I leave?" I chuckle, sliding my arm behind my head so I can see her better. I love that she has absolutely no modesty or shame about her body. She's completely naked, the blankets pooled around her waist, not an ounce of concern about covering herself. She does, however, fidget with those same covers, working the material between her fingers, before answering me.

"I don't know." She shrugs. "I didn't ask you to stay."

"You didn't ask me to leave either." I sit up, settling my palm on her cheek. "Did I overstay my welcome?"

"I love that you're still here, otherwise I wouldn't be able to do this." She uncrosses her legs and swings one over me, straddling my waist, my cock more than ready. Her mouth is against mine before I can speak, and for the next thirty minutes, I'm so fucking thrilled I stayed too.

"You're insatiable." I pant, as she rolls off me, with a cat ate the canary grin plastered on her face.

She lays on her side, her chin cradled in her hand as she leans on her elbow. "It's because you're so fucking delicious." Her fingers graze lightly back and forth over my torso. "Your body is a work of art."

My chest vibrates under her touch. "Isn't that what I'm supposed to say to you?"

"I don't need you to say that to me. I can feel it just in the way you look at me and touch me." She flattens her hand over my heart. "I don't deserve that kind of adoration, believe me."

I roll quickly, flipping her onto her back to lean over her. "You deserve that and more." I press my lips to hers in affirmation. When I pull away, she gives me a small smile.

"Don't make me fall for you. I'm not the kind of girl a guy like you should end up with."

"And what kind of girl is that?" I frown, looking her in the eyes.

"The wrong kind." Her voice is solemn as she stares back at me.

"Let me be the judge of that." I seal my mouth against hers, not wanting to hear another argument out of her, because I know I'm already falling for her, and any warning she wants to give me, would be on deaf ears. When her body finally relaxes underneath mine, I roll off her, pulling her with me as I rise from the bed. "Let's take a shower. I want to take you to my favorite breakfast place ever."

"You sure have a lot of favorite places you like to go eat." She mumbles as I tow her to the bathroom. "Wouldn't you rather just order room service and spend the day in bed?"

"You'll like this." I reach inside the shower stall to turn the water on. "Besides, I have someplace else I want to take you."

"Like a surprise?" Her face lights up as I tug her into the shower with me.

"Yep, just like that." Our wet lips fuse under the hot water pouring over us, a smile finally lifting her lips.

Fifteen minutes later, we're in her bedroom, her perusing the rows and rows of clothes hanging in her closet. "What should I wear?"

"Anything comfortable." I put the clothes on I wore the night before, but don't mind, as they really weren't on very long, to begin with. "Do you have coffee?"

She turns, grimacing, which tells me what her answer is going to be. "I can call room service?"

"Don't worry about it." I wave her concern off. "I'll wait out in the living room while you get ready." I head in that direction, stop as I pass to drop a kiss against her lips, then keep going.

Forty minutes later we're crossing over the Brooklyn Bridge, her brows arched high. "You're taking me to Brooklyn?"

"I'm taking you to my favorite breakfast place." I turn to flash my teeth at her. "Which just happens to be in Brooklyn."

"They better have the best damn food ever." She grumbles, turning to look out the window. If you're a Manhattanite, going to Brooklyn, or over any of the bridges that take you off the island, it better be for a good God damn reason, because to them, nothing can be better than it is on the island.

Another twenty minutes later, I find a parking spot and help her out of the car. It's a gorgeous Spring day, the temperature already nearing sixty degrees, so the short walk to the restaurant is refreshing. Her hand slips naturally into mine now whenever we're together, and I hope it means she's finally letting her guard down. When we reach the café, I pull the brightly painted door, labeled Barnyard Bistro, open so we can both enter.

"Cameron!"

The corner of my lips lifts into a huge smile as I turn toward the voice of my favorite waitress walking toward me. "Hey, Phoenix!"

"Nice to see you!" Her arms wrap around me in a quick hug. "It's been a long minute since we've seen you."

"Yeah, been crazy lately." We release each other. "This is my girlfriend, Gabby." I tug her hand to pull her closer.

"So nice to meet you." Phoenix leans over to give Gabby a quick hug. I chuckle at the dazed expression on Gabby's face, unsure if it's because of how I introduced her, or because of Phoenix's show of affection.

"You got a table for us?"

"Sure do." She swipes two menus off the counter behind her, then motions for us to follow her. She seats us at a table near the back of the café, up against a window, the warm sun shining in through the glass. "How's this?"

"Perfect, thanks." I pull Gabby's seat out for her, then sit across from her. Phoenix hands us our menus, takes our drink orders, then tells us she'll be back in a jiffy to take our orders.

Gabby opens her menu, holding it up in front of her face, muttering behind it at me. "She's awfully pretty. Are you related? She looks like she could be your sister, but then I'm probably not that lucky."

I place my finger on the top of her menu to push it down until I can see her face. "What are you grumbling about?"

"I was just saying she's quite pretty." She jerks the menu back up.

I pluck the menu out of her hands, her mouth gaping open at the action. "Are you jealous?"

She reaches over and tries to snag the menu back from me, but I move it behind my back where she can't reach it. She growls out loud and slams her palm flat on the table. "Give me my damn menu Cameron!"

I laugh out loud at her little tantrum. "You are." I shake my head, the smile on my face growing wider, which of course only causes her brows to draw together more tightly. "You're jealous."

She crosses her arms over her chest. "You just seemed very comfy and cozy with each other."

"She's friends with one of my sisters. They dance or paint or do some shit together, so I've known her for a few years." I lean across the table to put my hand over hers, threading my fingers through hers. "She's like a little sister to me. That's it."

Gabby peers across the table at me, her dark lashes blinking several times before she speaks. "I wasn't jealous."

I scoff loudly. "Alright, if you say so."

Her foot stomps under that table. "I wasn't. I was angry." She squints her eyes at me. "I thought you might have actually been dumb enough to bring me someplace an ex-girlfriend worked or something."

"Give me a little credit, Gabby." I squeeze her fingers. "Do I seem like the kind of guy who would pull a dick move like that?"

"I'm sorry." She mutters, then looks directly at me. "I seem to keep forgetting that you're one of the good guys."

I stare back at her for a moment, wondering not for the first time, who the hell did a number on her, then offer her a smile. "You're forgiven."

We enjoy a delicious breakfast after that, our conversation and mood much lighter after we have some caffeine and food in our bellies. We say our goodbyes to Phoenix after I pay the bill and head back outside.

As we stroll down the sidewalk, she points across and up the street. "Look, there's one of those inside flea markets." She turns to me, her eyes bright. "Do you mind if we go in and look around?"

"Sure, let's do it." We cross the street and enter the big warehouse to find rows and rows of vendor booths set up. There's something for everyone in this place. Booths with purses, jewelry, antiques, records, books, knick-knacks; you name it, it's in here. It's entertaining to watch the different expressions on Gabby's face with each new discovery she makes in every booth we enter, but none as much as the one she's making now.

"Oh my god! This is gorgeous!" She pulls a long green dress off a rack and spins around with it. "This would be perfect for next weekend!" She stops mid-spin and exclaims. "You need to come with me."

"Okay, I'll bite." I cross my arms and rock back on my heels.

She takes a step closer to me, still holding the dress up. "The annual hospital ball is next weekend. I was just going to go with Charlie, but would you like to go with me?"

"Why, Miss Reed, are you asking me to the prom?" I grin devilishly, remembering our conversation last night.

"Oh my God!" She throws her head back as she laughs. "This does feel like I'm asking you to the damn prom!" When she stops laughing she levels her eyes back to mine. "Do you have your daughter next weekend? Honestly, I'd love to have you go with me."

Closing the distance between us in one step, I wrap an arm around her waist then tug her against me, my lips landing on hers in a short, heated kiss. "I have Willow this weekend, so yes, I'd love to be your date for the ball."

"Yay!" She lifts up on the tips of her toes, presses her raised smile to mine, then wraps her arms, dress and all, around me.

She tries the dress on, and to her surprise, and mine, it fits her almost perfectly. She pays for it, insisting it's a steal at two hundred dollars, even though I argue I'd like to buy it for her. Honestly, she lost me somewhere after hand-sewn gems and vintage, so it was easier to just let her have her way and let her pay. Besides, I had one more place I wanted to take her this afternoon, and the sooner we paid, the sooner I could get her there.

"So, not one hint as to where you're taking me?" She pleads, bouncing in the seat next to me, reminding me very much of my six-year-old daughter at the moment, which I, of course, tell her. She flops back in her seat with a huff. "Well, if you tease her as much as you do me, it's no wonder!"

"We're almost there." I rest my hand on her thigh to squeeze it gently. "Ten more minutes."

She sits up straighter and looks around for a sign or clue out the window. "So it's in Brooklyn then?" She is not giving up without a fight. Two minutes later, she points to a billboard plastered on the side of a building, turning to me with a big grin. "Is that where we're going?"

I cock one side of my mouth up in a grin and nod, my insides warming when her smile widens. "When I saw your fish tank last night, I thought you might like it." I lift her hand and place a kiss against the back of her knuckles.

And she does. We spend the next two hours exploring the New York Aquarium, visiting each exhibit learning about the wonders of the sea. We both agree that the otters are the most fun to watch, as they seemed to find endless ways of causing trouble, even in an enclosed structure. I hope that at some point we can come back together, and bring Willow, but I keep that to myself, for now, not wanting to push too much too soon with Gabby.

The aquarium closes at three, so after the attendants are able to finally get us to leave, we make our way back to

Manhattan. As we cross over the Brooklyn Bridge, Gabby hugs my fingers gently. "Thanks for a really great day."

"It was a great day, wasn't it?" I glance at her, my heart warming to see genuine happiness radiating from her; my very own, beautiful mermaid that I somehow managed to find in this great big ocean.

CHAPTER
Eleven

~Gabrielle~

I moan, my back arching deliciously into the hand cupped around my breast, Cameron's hard length sliding between my ass cheeks. His other hand slips between my folds, his fingers rubbing under the hood of my clit, heat rushing to the already sensitive area.

"Oh my God, Cam." I mewl out, grinding my core into his touch. "Harder. Please." I spread my legs wider, and push my hips down, trying to shove his fingers inside me. He's faster than me though, and draws back, teasing me, clucking his tongue.

"Not yet baby." He whispers in my ear, then traces the length of my neck with his lips, nipping my shoulder lightly as his fingers do the opposite to my peaked nipple. His touch is soft and hard at the same time, my skin breaking out in goosebumps even though the blood rushing through my veins has never felt hotter.

I wrench my head back, searching for him. "Kiss me." I pant, demanding more of his touch. His mouth crashes against mine, my hand clasping onto the back of his head in a desperate attempt at keeping some control. He's stronger than me and tears his mouth easily from mine, snarling when I bite onto his lip. A smack lands hard against my ass and I yelp, my mouth parting, his lip pulling free as my eyes pop wide.

"You like that?" His hand kneads the spot now tingling, then lifts and lands on the same spot again, even harder. I practically cum from that alone, withering under his touch for more. "You want it harder?" He growls into my ear, his other hand fisting my hair, as I try to nod.

"Fuck yes." I beg, thrusting my ass back into his palm. His grip slides around my waist and hoists me up onto my knees instead. I balance myself on my elbows, looking over my shoulder as he lines up behind me, then shoves into me in one stroke, my body rocking forward from the force. I toss my head back, a guttural cry of pure pleasure rolling up from my lungs that echoes through the room when he slides back and plunges inside me again and again.

"Is this what you want?" He pants, his fingers dig into my sides, pinching my flesh in a way I know will bruise. I grunt my approval, welcoming the overwhelming feeling of being possessed by him. His hips piston against my ass, his cock driving deeper inside of me with every push, heaving into me. "You like it like this?"

"Yes, yes!" I gasp, bucking back to meet him, my insides starting to quiver, clenching around his length as he slams into me a final time, roaring out my name as I feel him explode inside of me, a scream leaving my lips as we tumble over the cliff into bliss together.

"Holy shit, Gabby." Cameron pants, rolling to lie beside me on the bed. "How am I supposed to ever leave if we keep doing that?"

I giggle, draping myself over his chest, loving the smooth expanse against my cheek as I lay there. "You've figured out my devious plan to make you my prisoner."

"Believe me, if I didn't have to pick Willow up from school in an hour, I'd happily stay." His hot lips drop kisses against my bare shoulder as I nuzzle into him, wondering how in the fuck I got here so quickly. This place where I actually want a guy to stay. Stay in my bed. Stay in my apartment. Stay in my heart. "Tell me again what your schedule is. You got me all distracted with your body again, so I can't remember."

His chest vibrates under my cheek as he begins talking. "I've got Willow tonight and tomorrow until five. I'm working tomorrow, then Sunday through Tuesday too. I'm off again on Wednesday."

I lift myself off his chest to look up at his face, sticking my lower lip out dramatically. "So, I have to wait until Wednesday to see you again?" I huff out an exaggerated breath as I drop back onto his chest. "That sucks."

His hands skim through my hair, tickling my back when his fingers trace over my skin. "I'll try to drop in to see you tomorrow night if it's not too busy. You're still on nights this week, right?"

"Yes, Saturday until Wednesday. Then I won't work again until the Monday after the ball, but back on days."

He hooks his hands under my arms to hoist me up his

body until my head is even with his. "We'll figure it out, okay? Don't worry."

His lips claim mine in a kiss. After a moment, I extract myself slowly, my voice low as I make an admission. "I don't really know how to do this."

"Do what?" His head tilts.

"You know, date." I shrug, looking down as I feel my cheeks heat. "I don't do relationships."

His finger slips under my chin, lifting it back up to meet his eyes. "But you want to, right?" He blinks when I don't respond. "Because you know this isn't normal. What's happening between us. What I'm feeling for you. It's different. It's special."

"I like you." I state, knowing it sounds too simple, but confused about how else to express how I'm feeling.

He chuckles, his smile calming the jitters quaking inside of me. "Yes, I hope so, seeing how you're lying on top of me naked."

"I just, I don't--" I giggle, even though I'm trying to maintain some level of seriousness. "It's not in my nature to like anyone, that's all. But I do. Like you."

"Well, as long as that's settled." He chuckles again, pushing me up with him as he shifts to sit. "Gabby, we'll figure it out." He leans forward, pulling me into a kiss that effectively ends our conversation, but on the best note possible.

Cameron left a little after two to go pick Willow up at school, but I'm still in bed, savoring his scent that still lingers on my blankets when my cell rings. I frown when I see who it is on the caller ID. "Hey, Cory."

"Hi, Gabrielle. Just confirming your date for this evening."

My heart plummets to the bottom of my stomach at the thought of having to go out on a date with another man, which tells me so much more about my feelings for Cameron than I'm willing to admit out loud. "Do you have the details?"

"I'll send them to your email. But it's one of your regulars, Jason Redding, so should be no surprises or anything like that for you."

"Cory, I may have a surprise for you actually." I retort quickly before I lose my nerve.

"Oh boy, I can't wait for this."

"This will be my last date. I'm going to have to leave Temptations." My heart beats double-time as I spit out the words and wait for her reaction.

There's a moment of silence, then a long sigh before she finally speaks. "You know you already have two scheduled dates for next week, and one of them is with the senator."

"Have Faith and Xander take care of the senator. Who's the other date?"

"It's someone new, so I can reschedule that one." She sighs again. "Are you sure Gabrielle? You're one of the most popular escorts on rotation. You'll be greatly missed by some of the clients."

I nod my head, even though I know she can't see me. "I'm sure. Thank you, Cory. For everything."

"Of course. Let me know if you ever want to come back." She hangs up without saying goodbye, but that's typical of her, so I don't take it personally. I throw the covers off me, slide out of bed, then fall back on my ass, landing on the edge of the mattress, a groan leaving me as I try to mentally prepare for the night ahead.

Several hours later, I step out of the car that Jason, the client, sent for me, and enter the lobby of the Sapphire Resort on Park Avenue. I'm meeting him in the rooftop restaurant, Blue Skies, which yes, I know, is yet another date conveniently located in another hotel.

I actually really enjoy the time I've spent with Jason in the past. He's a very attractive, single man in his late thirties that travels to Manhattan regularly on business. When he's in town, it's become routine for us to have dinner, and of course, because he was so good looking, sleeping with him had always been a no-brainer for me.

I take the elevator up to the restaurant, and upon entering, spot him so head in his direction. When he notices I'm approaching, his face lights up in a quick smile as he stands to greet me. "Elle, you look beautiful as always." Yes, that's right. He called me Elle. My friends call me Gabby, my parents and employers Gabrielle, but my dates know me as Elle.

I kiss him on the cheek and return the compliment. "Jason, so nice to see you again. It's been a little while."

He helps me into my chair, then sits beside me. "Yes, I've been in Europe for the last month closing a deal there. I was anxious to get back to the states." He slides his hand over mine and lowers his voice. "I've missed you."

And it's then, as my skin crawls at the touch of another man, that I realize I've fallen in love with Cameron. It's not the feeling of a thousand little legs scurrying over my body that spurs the epiphany. It's the absolute knowing that I only want it to be Cameron's hand on mine, his fingers lacing with mine, his skin against mine ever again.

"Elle, are you alright? You look pale." Jason reaches for his glass of water and places it in front of me. "Here, drink this."

I nod, grateful for the moment to collect myself and accept the water, taking several large sips. When I set the glass down, I slide my hand out from under his and place it in my lap as I look up at him. "I can't do this."

His brows furrow. "Do what?"

"I'm sorry Jason. I really am." I take another drink of the water. "I thought I could have dinner with you, spend some time with you, but I can't. I'm in love with someone else."

His brows shoot up. "Oh." He regains his composure quickly, his lips tilting up in a crooked smile. "I suppose there are much worse reasons for you wouldn't want to spend time with me. I think this is one I can definitely live with."

"You aren't angry?" Normally I couldn't give two shits if I made someone mad because I said no, but I really did enjoy the time I spent with Jason and didn't want to end things on a bad note.

"Not at all." He leans forward across the table, cupping my cheek in his hand. "He's a lucky guy. I hope he deserves you." Then he sits back in his seat, a warm smile on his face. "Do you still want to have dinner with me? Just dinner of course."

"Thank you." I rise from my seat. "But, no." I take a step closer to him to place a chaste kiss on his cheek. "You're the best Jason. Take care." And I leave, my heart a little fuller, my head a little clearer, and I think, foolishly, my life a little simpler.

CHAPTER
Twelve

~Cameron~

Willow and I spend some time in the park after I pick her up from school, then I take her to see a movie. I'm not going to lie, I fell asleep halfway through, but to be fair, little gnomes running around in squeaky voices didn't exactly do much to keep my attention. And the fact that Gabby kept me up most of the night before seemed to have finally caught up with me. After feeling like the worst parent in the world when Willow had to shake me awake, I take her to dinner at Graciela's, where she is treated like royalty and spoiled to death.

"Are you going to get a quesadilla or the taco's tonight?" We're seated at the table, chips, and salsa being munched between us.

"Quesadilla." She declares as she bites into a chip, then

frowns. "Daddy, I can't believe you fell asleep during the movie."

I cover my face and groan loudly. "I know!" I drop my hand. "Don't tell Mommy. She'll kill me. I guess I was tired."

"You missed the best part though. When the two little gnomes fall in love. It was so cute." She clasps her hands over her heart, a complete look of adoration on her face.

I chuckle. "Sorry, Bean. We can rent the movie when it comes out and I promise I'll stay awake next time."

"Okay." She takes a crayon from a can sitting in the center of our table and starts drawing little hearts on the paper tablecloth covering our table. I frown at what seems to be her new obsession with hearts and love, wondering when the heck this happened. She stops doodling and looks up at me. "Daddy, do you think you'll ever be in love again? Like you were with Mommy?"

Whoa. That was out of left field. They don't prepare you for shit like this when you have a kid. Especially when you get a divorce and have to figure out what to say that won't piss your ex off, and also have it make sense to a six-year-old. Gabby's face pops into my head and I smile, realizing maybe the time for this question is pretty timely. "I hope so honey. Would that bother you if I fell in love with someone else besides your mommy?"

She shakes her head emphatically, popping another chip into her mouth, crunching as she replies. "As long as you don't stop loving me too."

My breath is literally sucked from my chest as my heart stops. I lunge from my seat to pull her into my arms. "Never baby, never. Daddy will never, ever love anyone more than I love you."

Her little hands clasp around my neck as she hugs me back. "Then it's okay, Daddy. You can love someone beside Mommy."

I release my hold on her and move back to my own seat, staring in wonder at my daughter, who at only six, already has a heart so open and willing to love. I know I want to introduce Gabby to her, and this just made the decision even easier. We order, enjoy our dinner and then head home to my place where I tuck her in with wishes for sweet dreams.

Dropping her back off at her mom's house before my shift the next day always tears at my heart, but knowing she's loved by us both, helps. The void I feel when she's not with me though is hard, and dropping her off is a constant reminder that this is how it will always be. After hugs and kisses, she scoots across the sidewalk to her mom, and I head off for the precinct house. I've been off the last four nights, so I'm sure I have lots to catch up on and figure going in a little early will help with that.

Eight hours later, which included four doing paperwork, and three aggravated assaults, I'm frazzled and want a break. It's just after two in the morning, and hoping that maybe it will be quiet at the hospital, I let Brian know I'm going out for a bit. I don't text her, wanting to surprise her. Also, if I do notice it's busy, not disappoint her if I can't visit with her. I stop to grab some coffees as an excuse, then drive to the hospital. I have to press the buzzer to get in and wait for the doors to slide open before I can walk through.

Gabby's not at the triage desk tonight. I'm greeted by the nurse who was helping Gabby the night I brought the woman I found in the park. She smiles warmly in recognition when I explain who I am, then introduces herself as

Kinsley. She buzzes me in through the triage doors and tells me Gabby's out back doing patient checks if I want to go look for her. I leave the coffees with her and go in search of my little mermaid.

I turn the corner and smile when I see her leaning up against a wall, her back to me, speaking with another nurse. I lift my finger over my lips in the universal signal to 'be quiet' as the other nurse spots me, then sneak up behind Gabby, sliding my hands around her waist, as I press my lips against her neck.

"Trey, I thought I told you to stop doing that when Charlie wasn't around." She giggles, trying, unsuccessfully to get a rise out of me, then spins to face me, throwing her arms around my shoulders. "Hey handsome. This is a nice surprise!" Her eyes crinkle around the corners as she beams up at me.

"I missed you." I kiss her, pulling her flush, holding her tight for a minute.

"I missed you too." Her warm breath blows over my ear, before she steps back and out of my hold, turning her attention to the other nurse she was speaking to before I arrived. "Cameron, this is Jenny. Jenny, Cameron."

We exchange hellos, then Jenny excuses herself to go work on some charts. "Nice to meet you." I call out as she walks away with a wave over her shoulder.

"Come with me." Gabby grabs my hand and tugs me down the hall in the opposite direction. She stops in front of a door, swipes her keycard, then pushes it open, pulling me in behind her. As soon as the door shuts, she turns, shoves my body back against it, then crushes her mouth against mine. She locks each of her fingers around mine, slapping them back against the door beside my head, her body melting into mine as she makes me her prisoner. Her tongue sweeps over my lips until they part, lunging inside to curl around mine in need.

She tears her mouth from mine, her eyes wide and locked on mine as she issues another command, releasing the grasp she has on my hands. "Keep them there." I nod. My mouth kicking up on one side, interested to see where this is leading. She drags her short nails down the length of my chest, then stops when she reaches the belt at my waist. I feel her palm rest over the butt of my gun, her tongue swiping quickly along her bottom lip before she speaks. "Do you know how fucking hot it makes me when you wear a gun? Especially when I can see it on you?"

I tilt my head forward, nipping onto her lip, pulling it between my teeth for just a second before I release it to taste it with my tongue. "I think I have an idea."

I hear her releasing the buckle on my belt before I feel it, and glance down, moving my hands in that direction to stop her. She's quick though and slams my hands back up against the door. "I said keep them there." Her eyes slant in warning, then she drops to her knees to complete the task she started a second ago. Her fingers reach into my boxers to wrap around my thickening shaft, pulling it free.

"Gabby!" I hiss between clenched teeth. "What the fuck are you doing? Someone will hear."

She peeks up at me under her lashes, her cheeks flushed a light pink and smiles. "Then you better be quiet." One second later, I'm in her mouth, any further protest from me forgotten, the wet heat surrounding the head of my cock my only thought. Her nails bite into my ass as she sucks me into her throat, swallowing me deep, and I put my fist in my mouth to keep from groaning out loud. She slides back, her hand grasping around the lower part of my shaft, as her tongue swirls around the head of my cock. She drags the tip of her tongue slowly around the rim of my crown, the grip on her hand tight as she glides it up and down my length, before finally sucking it completely down her throat again.

"Fuck." I hiss out, my hips jerking against her mouth as she swallows again, gagging around me, her saliva coating my cock like silk. She works her fingers around me, matching the cadence to her head bobbing up and down. "So fucking good." I murmur, one hand dropping to the top of her head, petting her. She hums her approval, the vibration pushing me over the edge, my balls tightening a second before I come, her fist clenching around the base of my cock, my release sliding down her throat as she swallows. My breath is blowing out of me in short, gasping pants as I try to keep my knees from buckling under me as she drags her mouth off my dick and stands.

Her lips tilt up in the sexiest smile I've ever seen. "That was so much better than the coffee you brought last time." She licks around her lips with her tongue, her eyes glued to mine, and I swear, my cock twitches at the sight of it. What this damn woman does to me. I don't think I'll tell her I brought coffee because I agree, this is way fucking better.

"Guess I'll have to surprise you more often." I drawl, grazing my lips over hers.

"Anytime you want." She arches her brow suggestively. "These are the types of emergencies I like to handle."

"God, you're dirty, woman." I pull her against me and take her mouth in mine, not caring where it just was, only wanting to feel her close to me. Her arms snake around my neck, her fingers grasping onto my nape as she deepens the kiss, flinching when a loud rap sounds on the door underneath me.

"Gabs, we got a trauma coming in."

She giggles as she steps away from me, then yells back. "Be out it five." She waves her hand toward my mid-section, giggling again. "Put that away so I can get back to work detective!"

I roll my eyes, a huge grin plastered on my face, but do as she says, and buckle up my pants. "Want me to pick you up after work?"

"That would be amazing." She leans forward dropping a kiss to my lips, then grabs the handle by my hip to open the door. "Just no trips to Brooklyn for breakfast. I want to take you straight home to bed so I can have my wicked ways with you."

"Deal." I smack her ass as I stroll by her and head towards the exit. "See ya in a few hours, Princess."

CHAPTER
Thirteen

~Gabrielle~

"This feels very domestic to me." I scrunch my nose up as I stare at the Keurig coffee maker sitting on my pristine white kitchen counter. I point to two smaller square boxes stacked next to the machine. "And what are those? Do they need to be there?"

"Those are the coffee pods." He picks up one of the boxes, rips the top off, then dumps one of the pods into his palm. "Look." He lifts the handle on the Keurig, drops the pod in a slot, then closes the handle. He takes a coffee cup out of a cupboard, (*where in the hell did those come from*), slides it under the Keurig and presses a button. I jump when it whirs to life and starts drizzling coffee into the mug. He looks over at me to give me a cocky grin, which I just sneer at. A minute later he pulls the mug out from the dispenser and hands it to me. "Wa-lah! Your coffee madam."

I peer into the depths of the mug, then back up at him,

frowning. "There's no cream or sugar in it. It doesn't do that?"

He closes his eyes, shakes his head, muttering under his breath as he walks over to my refrigerator to pull the door open. He reaches inside, takes out a container of creamer and pours some into the cup. Next he tears open a single sugar packet that he plucks from a bowl on the counter, and dumps it in the cup. I finally smile, warmth spreading through me as I realize he remembers how I like my coffee. He really has thought of everything, but it's so much fun making him think that this is torture for me.

"See? Isn't it nice being able to make your own coffee? No calling room service, no waiting until we get to a coffee shop?"

"Well, it's definitely better than going to Brooklyn." I shrug, trying to hide my smile behind my mug as I take a sip. "And having you in my kitchen with your shirt off ain't so bad either."

He pulls the cup of coffee he just brewed for himself from the Keurig and wags a finger at me. "Don't get any ideas. I've got to get a run in before work if it kills me."

I slither up to him, and drag my fingers slowly down his torso, aiming for the waistband on his boxers. "I can think of a much better way to work out."

He stops me cold, grabbing my hand in his large one. "Listen you little minx, this body will not survive on sex alone, no matter how incredible it is." He chuckles, using the grip he has on my hand to yank me against him. "I will, however, meet you in the shower when I'm back if you want."

"Fine." I concede. "If that's the best offer you got." We

both grin playfully at each other as he drops a kiss to my nose then heads to my bedroom to change into his running clothes. It's late Tuesday afternoon, and we're both on at seven again tonight.

It's my last night shift for the next six weeks, and I would normally be thrilled. But knowing Cameron will still be on nights, and I'll be on days for those weeks, makes me wonder how we'll manage our time. He's picked me up the last two mornings after my shift and just slept here with me at my place. We haven't really talked about how we're going to spend our days and nights together once my schedule flips. Luckily, I'm off for the next five days, so as far as I'm concerned, he can stay anytime he wants, day or night, during that time, and we'll figure the rest out as we go.

As promised, when he returns from his run, we take a very naughty shower together, then get ready for work. My routine is easy; I slip on some nursing scrubs and twist my hair into a messy pile on top of my head. His is more complex. I sit on the toilet seat, talking to him while he shaves, both his face and his head. When that's done, he pulls a bottle of baby oil out of his bag and rubs it all over his body.

And hell yes, it's as sexy as it sounds, and no, he wouldn't let me help. But believe me when I tell you, that task will be performed by me sooner than later. I ask why he uses oil and not lotion, and he explains that colored skin gets really dry and ashy looking. The oil works best at keeping his skin soft and even looking. I can attest that it's working, and working well. Especially over the ridges of muscle that define his chest and stomach.

Anyway, from there, I follow him into my walk-in closet,

watching as he opens the garment bag he brought in this morning to pull out a dark gray suit. There's a sharp white dress shirt, a black belt, and matching shoes in the bag as well. Watching him dress is its own aphrodisiac. Yes, he's covering up, instead of getting naked, but damn if this man doesn't wear a suit well.

When he pulls his gun out of the holster to slide it through his belt, then shoves the gun back in after fastening his buckle, a dull ache throbs in my core. I don't know why, but the fact that he has the weapon on him at all times just does something to me.

"No tie?" I stand next to him, feeling extremely understated in my scrubs, inhaling deeply when he spritzes some cologne onto his neck.

"I hate ties." He slides his jacket on over his shoulders, squaring them off to settle the material in the right places. "Besides, I usually have my badge hanging around my neck, so it just gets in the way."

"Well, you look mighty fine, detective." I hum appreciatively as I drag my gaze over his sharply-dressed frame. "Tie or no tie, it doesn't matter."

He cocks up one side of his mouth in a crooked grin, gazing back at me. "You look gorgeous too. No matter what you have on."

"Well, wait to you see me in my dress on Saturday, then you can tell me how fabulous I look." I press a quick kiss to his lips, then slide my feet into my clogs. "You ready to go?"

"Yep, all set." He stops at my dresser, drapes his badge around his neck, stuffs his money clip into his pocket, and then follows behind me. Twenty minutes later, he drops me at the hospital with a kiss, then zooms off to the precinct house.

I'm working with Kinsley and Jenny again, and greet them both as I enter the emergency department. Jenny's got triage tonight, so Kinsley and I head out to the nurses' station out back to get up to speed on all the patients. The first half of the night flies by, trying to get the current patients discharged or admitted, on top of handling five new patients. I glance at the clock, noting it's just after one in the morning, and sigh, feeling like I've finally caught up enough to take a break.

I'm about to head to the cafeteria when Jenny calls out to me. "Gabby."

I spin on my heel, closing my eyes for just a second before I do, and turn in her direction. "What's up Jenny?" My brows furrow when instead of telling me, she motions for me to come closer.

When I'm less than a foot from her, she whispers to me. "There's a priest here, and he's got a badly beaten woman with him. He says you know her and that she only wants to see you."

"What?" Alarm sets my pulse racing as I brush past her to charge to the triage room, as I call behind me. "Did she say her name?" My feet freeze in place when I burst into the room my eyes landing on the bloody mess in the priest's arms. "Faith?" I look up at the priest for some kind of affirmation, which he gives, by nodding, his face as pale as his eyes are wide.

I slide to my knees beside her to check to see if she's conscious. "Faith, it's Gabby. Can you hear me?"

Her head barely moves, but she nods, fresh tears beginning to stream from her swollen lids. I take her hand in mine to cup it gently. "I'm going to help you, it's okay." I direct my attention to the priest. "Can you lift her? I need to get her to a room."

He stands, rising easily as he cradles her in his arms. "Just show me where."

I motion for him to follow me, and lead him to the first empty room I see, Jenny already waiting. "Go get Scott." He's the doctor on duty tonight, and there's no doubt in my mind that he needs to see my friend immediately.

The priest is already placing her gently on the bed when I turn my attention back to them, fury rolling through me when I see Faith flinch in pain. I grab an IV kit off the cart and sit next to her. "Faith, I'm going to set up an IV so I can give you something for the pain, okay?"

"Okay." She whimpers. I glance up at the priest, noting how he has his hand wrapped around her other hand.

"She's a regular at my church. I found her outside on the steps when I went to lock up after midnight mass."

"Did she say who did this?" I work while I talk; clean an area on the back of her hand, find a vein, insert the catheter, then tape it, securing it. I grab a bag of saline and connect the tube to the catheter, setting a steady drip to try and get some fluids into her to help avoid shock.

"No, she wouldn't tell me anything." He shakes his head, frowning as he looks down at her. "She didn't even want me to bring her to the hospital, and would only go if I promised to bring her to see you."

"You did the right thing." I stride to the med cabinet, swipe my card to unlock it, then grab a vial of morphine. Depending on the doctor on duty, we're given standing orders to administer certain medications as needed to a patient. There's no doubt she needs something for her pain immediately. "She definitely needs a doctor." I'm at her side again. "Faith, I need to know if you're allergic to anything? Can I give you morphine?"

She shakes her head slowly back and forth, whispering her reply through broken lips. "No allergies."

I do a quick blood pressure reading to make sure she's not bleeding internally, then don't waste another second, pushing a dose of the medicine directly into her IV, wanting to comfort her in any way I can right now. "This will help the pain, okay honey?" I squeeze her hand as I detach the vial, her body already growing limp as I do.

"What do you have?" Scott, the physician assistant on duty tonight, demands as he enters the room.

"Female, mid-twenties, badly beaten, found by this gentleman outside his church. Just administered two milligrams of morphine, have her on a saline drip, BP is 128/90."

Scott nods and lowers his voice. "Violated?"

I lift my shoulders, my lips pursing. "I don't know. But Scott, she's a friend."

He nods once, then turns his attention to Faith to begin his exam. I step back from the bed and direct my attention to the priest. "I'm sorry, I didn't get your name?"

"Father Noah Thomas."

"Well, Father Noah Thomas, I'm going to need you to step out of the room while we exam Faith, okay?" He inclines his head forward, then bends further, placing a kiss onto Faith's forehead, after saying some kind of prayer over her. When he rises, I direct him to the waiting area and let him know I'll update him as soon as I can.

I hold Faith's hand the entire time Scott exams and treats her, trying to make sure she feels as safe as she can. We ask her if she was sexually assaulted, and she tells us no, but Scott and I both stare up at each other when he turns the UV light on over her body.

Bright splatters glow across her upper thighs between her legs, the reaction that semen and other bodily fluids has when exposed to that type of light. Scott steps away from Faith to pull me aside. "She's saying she wasn't sexually assaulted, but this would indicate otherwise."

"God damn fucking bastard that did this to her." I hiss out, my teeth clenched.

"We'll need to call the police." He continues quietly, ignoring my anger. "She'll need a full panel of blood work including all STD checks, see if she needs or wants the morning after pill and if you can convince her, a rape kit."

"Jesus, Scott, any more good news?" I sigh, rubbing my forehead in frustration.

"Well, I don't think anything is broken, but just to be safe, it's probably a good idea to get a full set of x-rays on her ribs and face."

I nod, agreeing we should definitely cover every base. "Okay. I'll get started on everything. I just need to make a phone call. Could you go ask Jenny to come in? I don't want to leave her alone with you." I frown, knowing he understands that any woman in her condition would most likely be afraid to be left alone with a man, but feel the need to apologize anyway. "I'm sorry, Scott.

"It's not a problem." He pats my arm. "I'll call up and order the x-rays while I'm out there."

"Thanks." When Jenny shows up, I let Faith know I'll be back, and then dart out of the room. I pull my cell out of my pocket as I reach the hallway and call Cameron's cell; something I've never done before on shift.

"Hey princess. You calling for a coffee run?"

"Cam, you need to come down here. Another girl has been beaten. And maybe raped too." My voice catches as I say the last two words.

"Shit. Okay." I hear him take a deep breath. "I'll grab Brian and head over."

"Cameron?" I can hear him telling Brian they need to head my way.

"Yeah, I'm here."

"She's a friend." I blink, trying to keep my tears at bay. "She's my friend, and she's really hurt."

"Jesus, okay." I can hear him walking as he speaks to me. "Are you okay?"

"Just get here." I plead.

"On my way."

I end the call and head back to Faith.

CHAPTER
Fourteen

~Cameron~

"Wait here." I order Brian, then take a deep breath as I slowly push the door to the victim's room open, not wanting to startle or alarm her if she's sleeping. I instantly recognize the mass of dark curls piled on the head of the person sitting next to the bed. I mouth a silent hello when her head swings around. She leans down and speaks something quietly into the victim's ear, then gets up and motions for me to follow her out of the room.

As soon as the door closes behind us, she folds her arms around my chest, clinging tightly as her body falls into me. Her voice is muffled as she speaks against my shirt. "Cameron, it's awful what someone did to her. I wouldn't even have known it was her if I wasn't told."

I wrap my arms around her thin frame, holding her to

me until I feel her shift to look up at me. "Thank you for coming."

"Of course." I step back, putting a little space between us so it's easier to talk but hold one of her hands in mine to maintain our connection. "I wish it was for any other reason. I'm sorry." I turn my head to my partner, who has stepped a few feet away from us down the hall. "You remember Brian?"

"Of course." She gives him a small wave. "Hey."

"How is she?" I ask.

She bows her head, dragging her fingers across her cheek before raising it to speak again. "No broken bones, which is good. And she says she wasn't raped, but she did have consensual sex just prior."

"With the man that beat her?"

She shakes her head. "No. She said she was grabbed after she was leaving a date."

"A john?"

Her brows crease as she crosses her arms. "A date. She's not a hooker."

"Oh, I thought you called because she met the same criteria as the other women who were beaten."

"I called you because my boyfriend is a New York City detective, and she's my friend, so I thought you could help her." Her hands ball into fists as she drops them to her sides.

"Gabby," I soften my approach, "Of course I'll do whatever I can for her. I'm sorry if I misunderstood the situation."

She stares at me for a long second, then speaks again. "She's an escort. So, there could be a connection."

"So, she is a hooker?" I challenge, confused as hell at the difference.

"An escort is not a hooker, Cameron." She blows out an exaggerated breath before continuing. "A hooker stands on a street corner and climbs into any dick's car for a measly fifty bucks. An escort is a highly paid professional who accompanies a person to a dinner, or a function, or a party, not to have sex. Quite different."

"But didn't you just say she had sex prior to being attacked?" I drag a hand over my head as I try to piece all the fragments she's giving me together.

"Argh." She stomps a foot on the floor. "She was with someone, sexually. A date. Not as an escort. When she was leaving that date, she was attacked. But the fact that she is an escort, professionally, does give her some kind of connection to the other attacks." She lifts a hand and waves it in front of me, like everything she's telling me should be crystal clear. "Get it now?"

I raise my brows and shuffle back a few steps as I nod. "Got it." I turn to point toward the door. "Can Brian and I talk to her?"

"Could just you go in?" She shuffles her feet, her eyes darting toward the door. "She's been violated enough for one evening. It might make it easier if only one man is present in the room."

"Of course." I nod, understanding completely. Normally in a situation like this, women officers would be present to make the victim feel safer, more comfortable. I was only here because Gabby called me directly. "Let me just explain to Brian."

She nods, and I step down the hall to speak to Brian, letting him know the situation. He understands of course, advising he'll wait out in the lobby in the meantime. I stride back to Gabby, who's waiting outside the door to the room, her hand pressing flat against my chest to stop me before entering. "Faith." She tilts her head to lock her gaze onto mine. "Her name is Faith." She blinks, waiting for me to acknowledge I've heard her, then continues. "She's on morphine for the pain, so she's groggy and may not be able to tell you much until later."

"Okay. I'll be respectful of that." I assure her, as she pushes the door open to enter the room.

She walks to the bedside and takes Faith's hand in hers. "Faith, there's someone here that would like to talk to you."

Faith's eyes flutter open, her tongue snaking out to drag slowly against her cracked lips. I move beside the bed to grab the cup of water off the table, and I offer the straw to her. "Here, this should help."

Her lips close around the straw and she sucks, the water sliding up into her mouth, her eyes closing again for a second when she swallows. When her lids open again, she nods her head, her lips lifting the tiniest fraction. "Thank you."

"Faith, this is Cameron Justice, the one I told you about." Gabby twists her head in my direction for a second, then turns back to her. "He's going to ask you a few questions if you're up to it."

She blinks several times as she digests Gabby's words, then gives another slight nod of the head. "Okay."

"Okay, I'm going to be right outside if you need anything." She bends to place a soft kiss on her friend's forehead, then leaves the room, giving my hand a squeeze as she walks by me.

I pull up a chair that's against the wall and move it

beside her bed to sit down. Her eyes follow my movements, more aware than I was expecting given Gabby's warning about the morphine. "Faith, I'm not sure if Gabby told you, but I'm a detective with the NYPD."

"She told me." Her cheeks lift in an attempt at a bigger smile. "And that you're dating."

I smile back. "Yes, that too." I shift my glance away for a second, then look back. "Did she also tell you that there have been other attacks similar to this over the last few weeks?"

"Yes, but detective, I think I know who did this."

My posture stiffens as my brows arch high. "I'm listening."

"I have a regular client." She scrunches her eyes closed for a second, swallows roughly, then continues, "but it's not him. I believe it's someone who works for him. But detective, it's extremely important to me that my client's identity is kept a secret."

"We'll obviously do everything we can to make sure that happens. Can you tell me why?" I offer her another drink from the glass, and she nods, taking a small sip from the straw.

"He's in public office." She lifts her hand, making a brushing motion. "But also because these people hire me because I'm discreet, and to keep their privacy. This shouldn't have to bounce back on him if he knows nothing about it."

"Of course." I nod. "Let's start with why you think you know who it is." I prod gently.

Her nostrils flare wide as her head shakes back and forth, a grimace on her lips. "His smell. I've always hated the cologne he wears. When he grabbed me to drag me into the alley, he had me pressed against his chest and it's all I could smell."

"Unfortunately, if it's a cologne that's marketed to the general public, that may not be enough."

"There's more." She shifts on the bed, trying to scoot her body up, her teeth crunching together from the discomfort. "Even though he tried to disguise his voice, I recognized it. And he called me Faith. More than once. How would he know my name unless it was someone I knew?"

"What kinds of things did he say to you?"

She closes her eyes, her brow furrowing then begins repeating things from memory. "I'm so done with whores like you Faith. You think going to church makes you clean Faith. Tired of your pussy in my world Faith." She opens her eyes slowly, a tear trickling from the corner of one.

"I'm sorry." I pull several tissues out of the box on her bed stand and hand them to her. "I know this isn't easy. I appreciate all the effort it takes to have to relive those moments."

Her mouth turns down, her eyes focusing on her fingers that are clenched around the sheet covering her. "It certainly seems he was right about the church. God didn't seem to be looking out for me at all. Maybe this was my punishment."

My lips press together tightly in a line, my fingers clenching onto the pen in my hand. "No. No one deserves this." I make sure she's looking at me as I continue. "Sometimes the hand of the devil is stronger than God's, but I truly believe God does everything he can to protect us when he can."

She nods slowly, wanting to agree with me, but I can tell by the frown on her face that she probably doesn't.

"Can you tell me the name of the person you think it is?" I press on, knowing she has to be exhausted.

"Steven Bennett." Her hands fist together in her lap. "He's Senator Martin Landon's personal assistant." She looks directly at me then, her eyes crystal clear. "I have absolutely no doubt that it was him."

"When was the last time you saw the senator?"

"Last night."

"Was Steven Bennett there?" I continue questioning.

"Yes, through dinner. But after-" she pauses, her cheeks flushing red even through her bruises, "when I spend private time with the senator, he leaves."

"Where does he go?"

"I have no idea. He just disappears and we usually don't see him again."

"We?" My head cocks.

She takes a deep breath, her eyes darting back down to her hands. "There's usually two of us with the senator. Last night it was another escort from the service."

I let that sink in, wanting to question her further about her extra-curricular activities as part of the service and if they are aware. Prostitution is illegal in the state of New York. But I have a bigger issue here with someone attacking people, and, if her attacker is connected to the others that have happened in recent weeks, that's more important. I let out a short sigh. "What's her name? We'll want to make sure she's not his next target."

"*His* name is Alexander Walker. Xander." She murmurs.

Well, shit, I wasn't expecting that, but hey, whatever floats his boat.

I question her for another ten minutes, trying to determine if there are any other dates scheduled with him in the future. I also ask if she knows any of the other victims, telling her their names, and finally, if she'd be willing to pick him out of a line-up if necessary. She was everything I could want in a perfect witness, and I was hopeful that we might actually have some kind of a lead. I wasn't certain there was a connection yet, but it gave us a place to start. After I thank her, I give her my card and let her know I'll be in touch.

When I leave the room, Gabby is waiting right outside the door for me. I smile tiredly. "Hey."

"How is she?" She closes the distance between us, her hands grasping onto the lapels of my jacket as she looks up at me.

"She did really good. I think she gave us some really good information to go on." I tilt forward to press my lips to her forehead in a kiss. "I've got to find Brian and head back to the precinct so I can pull all the pieces together. Did you pull DNA samples from her? Any hair, fingernail residue?"

She steps back from me, stuffing her hands into the front pockets of her scrubs as she does, and nods. "Yes, of course."

"Okay, good." I reach my hand out and cup her cheek, raising her face to look at mine. "Hey, I know this is hard." I pull her back to me. "We'll get this guy, I promise."

Her lips purse into a tight smile. "You better."

"I have to go." I lean into her, pressing my lips to hers in a long kiss. "I'll pick you up at seven, okay?"

"Okay." She captures my mouth for one more kiss, then walks me out front to find Brian, so I can head back to the precinct.

CHAPTER
Fifteen

~Gabrielle~

My skin prickles as an icy wave surges through me, my hand pressing against my stomach as bile rises in my throat when I hear the name Faith tells Cameron. *Steven fucking Bennett?* I always knew something was off with that guy, but never suspected he was capable of this kind of behavior. Why? That was what I couldn't figure out. Why would he want to hurt Faith? And the other women as well, if he had also beaten them?

I'm already formulating a plan in my head, knowing there is no way in hell I'm going to let him get away with what he did to Faith. If I have to trap him myself I will. The conversation I had with Cory the other day spins on replay in my head.

"You know you already have two scheduled dates for next week, and one of them is with the senator."

"Have Faith and Xander take care of the senator."

Could this have been me here instead of her? There's only one way to find out. I've already made the decision to call Cory to have her set up a date with the Senator next week. I'll tell her I want to have one more date with him so I can say goodbye properly. My treat to him. Because if I know anything about the legal system, even if they do get Steven Bennett in their clutches, it generally doesn't take much for someone like him to squirm his way out. I plan on making sure that doesn't happen.

I push back off the door when I hear Cameron say goodbye to Faith, and slump against the opposite wall, trying to make it appear as if I've been waiting patiently for him. We talk for a few minutes about Faith, and then I walk him out so he can go back to the precinct. After he leaves, I go back to spend more time with my friend, who's finally asleep. I stay anyway, holding her hand. I whisper promises to her about making this right, and about how sorry I am that this happened to her. It probably should have been me. And I'm bigger and stronger. Maybe I could have fought back. I stay for a half-hour then reluctantly get back to work.

As promised, Cameron is waiting for me outside the hospital when my shift ends. I never thought I would be the kind of girl who would be happy to have a man waiting for her. Knowing he's there, wanting to be just with me, gives me a level of comfort I didn't even know I craved. We're both exhausted, and after a shower, climb into my bed, into each other's arms and sleep for the next ten hours.

It's late Wednesday afternoon by the time we wake up, and even though we're both supposed to be off until Monday, Cameron tells me he wants to go into the office for a little while.

"But couldn't you go in tomorrow instead? I was really hoping we could go out somewhere together and get a nice dinner. I haven't spent any real time with you since last week." I take a sip of the coffee he made for me and wait for his response.

"I just really want to go over everything while it's fresh in my mind. This could be the break in the case that we've been waiting for." He sidles up beside me at the counter and bumps his hip into mine. "We've got all weekend to spend together, and the ball on Saturday too."

"I know." I pout, my shoulders sagging. "I understand. I do." I turn to face him. "Are you going to work all night?"

He shrugs, then skims a hand down my side, gripping onto my waist to tug me flush against his body. "If I promise to make it up to you, can I come back when I'm done?"

"Will you bring your handcuffs?"

His hand snakes around to cup my ass, holding it firm as he rocks his hips forward, his arousal hard against my core. "If you're not careful, I'll use them right now to keep you my prisoner until I come back."

I arch my back, rubbing my aching center against him, warm desire pooling between my legs at the very thought of him controlling me. "Don't tease me, Cameron." I reach up and snag his lower lip in my teeth, then drag my tongue over it when I let go. "It's not nice."

"If anyone's a tease woman, it's you." His hand smacks hard against my ass, his lips dropping against mine in a quick kiss before he pushes me gently off him. "I'm never going to leave if we keep this up."

I tilt my head and give him a coy smile. "You can't blame a girl for trying."

"You don't make it easy." He plants another kiss on my lips, then strides out of the kitchen. I don't end up seeing him again for two more nights, his excuse being work. I try to keep myself busy with Charlie, and visiting Faith, but hate that I feel a sense of loss at not seeing him. I'm falling hard, and it's all new to me. He seems to have no problem being away from me, so I'm also afraid that he's not feeling the same as me. We have talked on the phone and shared quite a few texts, but it's not the same. He said he'll definitely see me again on Saturday for the ball, so I'm counting down the days until then.

"Seriously, Gabby, that dress is absolutely gorgeous. I can't believe you found it at a flea market."

I'm at Charlie's, helping her get ready for the ball, and spin around to give her the full effect of the full skirt on the dress. "I know. Who would have thought I'd ever buy a used dress? But to be fair, I do believe it's vintage."

"Who cares? It's amazing on you." She rubs her ever-expanding stomach and groans. "What the hell was I thinking? Wearing a gray dress? I look like a damn whale in it!"

"Stop it!" I walk over to give her a hug. "You look beautiful. You're glowing. And I don't know any whale in history that could make chiffon look this dazzling."

"You have to say that, you're my best friend." She grumbles, then blows air into her cheeks puffing them out before releasing it in a big huff. "A big, fat, blow whale!"

"I'm gonna kick your ass if you say that again." I grab her hand to yank her away from the mirror she's staring in to. "Enough!" I continue tugging her out of the bedroom. "Come on, Trick is finally here, so we can leave."

Patrick, also known as Trick, his pilot call name in the army, is Trey's best friend. He lives one floor up from Charlie and Trey and is serving as Charlie's date tonight because Trey has to cover at the hospital. There's a bit of history between us, and not one I want to have to explain to Cameron, so I smile when I see them both sharing a beer and talking casually. I actually met Trick about a year ago in a bar. He helped me to secretly set Charlie up with Trey. Trick and Trey both worked at Temptations at the time. I spent more than a little time with Trick between the sheets, most of it amazing, and started working at Temptations because of him. We've remained friends, but one of my favorite things in the world to do is to give him a hard time any chance I can.

"Hey asshole, did someone actually teach you how to use a razor? I almost didn't recognize you." I give him a cheeky smile, and nudge his shoulder with mine as I move to stand between him and Cameron.

"Yeah, and I thought they only allowed ladies to wear nice dresses like that?" He arches a brow as his gaze skims down my body, then glances over at Cameron. "I hope you know what you got yourself into with this one."

Cameron slides his arm around my waist, pulling me into him. "My eyes are wide open." His lips press for a second against my bare shoulder. "Best damn thing I've gotten myself into in a long while."

Trick barks out a laugh, clapping Cameron on the shoulder. "Good for you man." He gives Cameron a genuine smile, then moves to gather the rest of us up to leave. We pile into the car Trey hired for us and arrive at the ball around thirty minutes later. We follow the crowd to the ballroom and then look around for a table to settle at, picking one between the dance floor and the bar. Cameron and Trick leave to get us a round of drinks, leaving Charlie and I to gossip and fawn over all the different gowns women are wearing.

"Here you go, ladies." Cameron places a tumbler of tequila on the rocks in front of me, and a club soda with a splash of cranberry in front of Charlie. Trick hands off the extra beer he was holding to Cam, and then they both sit down next to us.

"God, you have no idea how much I miss a good drink." Charlie stares at my glass, her lips pursed in a frown.

"Come on preggers," Trick stands up and holds his hand out to Charlie, "let's go dance instead then."

I smile, wishing more people could experience the sweet side of Trick that he keeps hidden so well, watching as he escorts her out to the floor and sweeps her around in his arms. "He's an interesting guy." Cameron says, jostling me out of my thoughts.

I turn to him. "Yeah, he's okay. Has a tough history. Once you get to know him, he's not so bad." I scoot in my seat so I'm closer. "But let's talk about you. Have I told you how insanely handsome you look in that tuxedo?"

His finger latches under the bow tie and tugs, his tongue sticking out for a second. "I feel like I'm being strangled, but for you, it's totally worth it."

"Don't worry, I plan on having you out of that tux very

soon." I wink, sucking my lower lip between my teeth as I tilt my head, making sure my intentions are clear.

"Come on." He stands, pulling me up with him. "I want to dance with you. I mean, you did take lessons after all. Let's put them to use." He grins across at me as we make our way to the dance floor, his arms wrapping around me once we're there.

I rest my chin in the crook of his neck, the scent of him seeping into my nostrils every time I inhale. "I've missed you." I mumble against his skin.

His arms tighten around me, his lips soft against my ear. "I've missed you too." He squeezes me again. "So much. More than I realized until I saw you tonight." He sways us back and forth, one hand pressed against the small of my back, the other around my shoulders. "Every time I see you again for the first time, my heart almost stops at how much more beautiful you get."

"Cameron." I whisper, turning my head so I can look at him. "You're going to make me fall in love with you." His gray eyes lock onto mine, holding them in a long stare before he finally speaks, his voice low. "You already made me fall in love with you." He claims my gaping mouth in a delicate kiss, ceasing any further discussion on the matter, my heart fluttering madly against my chest. When he breaks his hold, he pulls me close again to whisper in my ear. "Don't say anything. Just dance with me."

CHAPTER
Sixteen

~Cameron~

Is it normal for a guy's cock to get hard after he confesses he loves someone? That's the thought running through my mind as I continue dancing with Gabby, using her body as coverage to hide my erection. She makes me feel things I never have before, so I guess this reaction shouldn't be too surprising. It is rather embarrassing however, that a man my age can't control his own damn dick. Not that it's a problem for Gabby.

"Hmmm, I can feel you're packing at least one weapon tonight." Her hot breath murmurs against my ear as she eases her hips a little closer to mine. "We can leave anytime you'd like."

"Always the naughty girl, aren't you?" I growl back, actually loving her suggestion, but feeling somewhat obligated to stay a bit longer for Charlie and Trick.

Her tongue sweeps across the lobe of my ear, a chill

tingling down my neck as she purrs in response. "I think that's just the way you like me."

I twist my head to hers, capturing her mouth in mine, a small gasp escaping right before I seal my lips over hers, desperate for even a small taste of her. When I break away, her hungry eyes latch onto mine, her need as apparent as mine. Neither of us says a word as I gather her even tighter against my body, the heat between us reaching molten levels. When the song ends, I keep an arm wrapped against her waist, tethering her to my side, not wanting her touch gone for even a second.

Food is being served as we reach the table, and we both sit, grateful for some kind of distraction to the lust steaming between us. During dinner, we make easy conversation with Charlie, Trick and some other friends from the hospital that the girls are acquainted with. Dessert is a delicious trio of heaven on a plate, consisting of a mini crème brulee, tiramisu, and berries with cream. Charlie had hers, as well as Trick's, using the age-old excuse of eating for two, but in her defense, the poor girl couldn't even enjoy a cocktail, so more power to her.

"I'm going to go to the bar for an after-dinner drink." Trick announces, getting up from the table. "Anyone else?"

I shake my head no, already feeling a slight buzz from the several beers I've had, but Gabby stands and nods. "I'll go with you."

I immediately rise next to Gabby. "I can go." I pull her chair out for her. "You sit."

"I'm fine Cam." She gives me a wide smile and pats my arm. "You keep Charlie company for me."

I watch as Gabby catches up to Trick, who's already

standing in line for the bar. My teeth clench when she slides an arm around his waist and leans into him. They seem too familiar, too friendly, triggering a red flag in my gut. Charlie must sense my reaction because she's suddenly sitting next to me, her hand draping over mine warmly. "They're just friends."

I scoff, slightly embarrassed and give her a lopsided grin. "That obvious?"

She offers me a small shrug and matching smile. "She's gorgeous, he's got that ruggedly handsome thing going for him, they look pretty cozy over there in line. I get it."

"So nothing to worry about?" I ask, feeling like a fucking pussy the second after the words leave my mouth.

"They had a little thing." Her eyes dart in their direction, then back to me. "Maybe a year ago." My brows furrow at the new information, my stomach seizing at the thought of Gabby with him, with anyone else but me. "But Cameron, I've never seen her this happy before. This content. Gabby doesn't do relationships, and she's steaming full ahead with you." My insides relax a little at this additional information. "You've got absolutely nothing to worry about. She's crazy about you."

"The feeling is mutual." I admit, my cheeks lifting in a smile as Gabby returns and sits beside me.

"You two look awful serious." She takes a sip of her drink as she looks between us.

"Just warning Cameron that he better take good care of my bestie." Her nose scrunching up as she gives us both a wide smile. "Did you lose Trick?" Charlie peers over our shoulders. "Let me guess, saw someone he couldn't resist?"

"He definitely saw someone." Gabby leans over the table,

her voice lowering as she continues. "There was some brunette in a red dress at a table behind us who ran off when she saw Trick, and then he ran off after her."

"Ooooh, I wonder who it is?" Charlie coos out curiously, both of the girls faces light up over the mystery.

"Don't know." Gabby states. "But I have a feeling you may have just lost your date."

Charlie stretches her spine as she sits upright, her hand landing on top of her baby bump. "That's fine with me actually, I'm more than ready to leave. How about you guys?"

Music to my fucking ears. I consent without even checking with Gabby. "I'm happy to go whenever you ladies are."

Charlie stands, widening her stance to get her balance, then rolls her eyes. "Good lord, who knew getting up was going to get hard too. Wait 'til you do this Gabby."

"Uh, yeah, don't think we have to worry about that." I state, very matter-of-factly.

"That's what I said." She starts waddling away. "I'll go find Trick and let him know we're leaving."

"Okay." Gabby and I both sing out in unison, then look at each other and laugh. I turn my face to hers as I continue to chuckle. "We're not anxious or anything, huh?"

"Speak for yourself." She places both her hands flat on my thighs, then slides them slowly toward my groin as she pushes her body forward. "I can't fucking wait to leave."

"Jesus, woman, that mouth is dirty." I growl, leaning into her, nipping her lower lip. "I can't wait to get you home."

"Let's go find Charlie and get our coats." Her fingers dig into my legs as she presses against them to stand, her hair flipping over her shoulder as she grabs my hand to lead me to the exit. We run into Charlie on our way, who informs us that Trick was in some hot and heavy conversation with the brunette and told her that he'd find his own way home. The ride back to Charlie's is filled with theories and gossip about the mystery woman, but at least it's quick, and I blow out a sigh of relief when we're finally alone in the car.

"Alone at last." I grin wickedly, my fingers working to bunch the long fabric of the skirt up over her knee, allowing my hand to slide underneath. Her eyes dart to the front of the car towards the driver, her legs spreading wider when she's satisfied he's not watching. *This*. This is why this woman fascinates me, holds me as a willing captive. Any other woman would have snapped their legs closed and brushed my hand away, but not her. She invites me in, dares me to take her anywhere or anyplace I want. And I accept, my length thickening as I skim my way up the inside of her thigh, not stopping until my fingers bump up against soft silk.

She arches her hips just a fraction forward as I flatten my hand, cupping it over her pussy, her center already warm and damp. I apply pressure to just my middle finger, pushing the silk into her folds, then drag my finger back and forth, the material soaking through almost immediately. Her hand clamps down onto my upper thigh, her nails biting through the material of my trousers into my skin as she sucks in a breath.

I smirk, loving for once that I have her squirming. I slide my ring finger in to join my middle, her core throbbing around them, her wetness leaking onto them. Her mouth opens in a small O, and before a sound can escape, I clamp my mouth over hers, my tongue darting inside to find hers.

She tastes like tequila and lime and heat as we devour each other, our need for each other all consuming.

Her grip on my thigh has relocated to my aching length, a moan catching in my throat when she strokes it roughly. It's her way of showing me that two can play at this game. I'm so up for the challenge, swiping under the soaked material of her panties, my fingers finding, then flicking her clit. Her teeth clamp hard onto my bottom lip, yanking on it until I slide my hand out from under her skirt. She releases her grip, my head snapping back an inch, our eyes locking together. I lift my wet fingers and trace them over the outline of her lips, our gaze still locked, her hand still rubbing my shaft, then slam my mouth back over hers, the taste of her exploding against my tongue.

My whole body is on fire, my balls tingling as they begin to tighten, and I rip away from her, snatching her hand off my cock before I come, my breathing ragged. She's only inches from me, and giggles softly, a devilish tone accompanying it as she grins. "I win."

I tilt my head, my brows arching. "You think-"

The driver clears his throat loudly in front of us, smart enough not to turn around, interrupting my rebuttal. "Sir, Miss, we've arrived."

I swing my attention in his direction. "Perfect timing." I move to open my door, surprised when it's pulled open by one of the hotel staff.

"Good evening, Sir." The smartly dressed gentleman addresses me. "Dinner with us this evening?"

"We're staying." I reach in, extending my hand to Gabby, who slides elegantly out of the car after clasping it.

The man's face brightens with recognition. "Oh, Miss Reed, I didn't realize the gentleman was with you."

She offers him a polite smile. "No problem Phillip." Then swings her glance to me, a twinkle in her eye as she continues. "As Mr. Justice stated, we'll be staying in the rest of the evening, thank you."

She practically drags me into the lobby, the traction she's getting in four-inch heels extremely impressive, only to stab the call button numerous times impatiently when the doors don't open immediately.

"In a hurry?" I drawl, leaning casually against the wall as I watch her.

She whips her head in my direction, stomps the three steps it takes to stand before me, her heels clicking loudly on the marble floor as she does. Her hands ball into fists on her waist as she glares up at me, hissing. "Yes, I'm in a hurry! I'm in a big, god damn hurry to have you bury your big, hard cock in me!"

The doors swish open, and before she can react, I grab her around the waist, sling her over my shoulder. I smack her on the ass for good measure, chuckling as I step into the elevator. "Who won, Miss Reed?"

"Oh my god!" Her hands clutch onto the back of my jacket, as she tries to wriggle off of my shoulder. "Cameron put me down!"

"Nope." I tighten my hold, when she squirms harder, strolling off the elevator when it reaches her floor. I have her room key in my pocket, so I pull it out and swipe it over the sensor, kicking the door open when the lock releases. I stride straight for her bedroom, tossing her onto the bed, lean over her on my arms to lock her in, and grin wickedly. "Now, where did you want my big, hard cock?"

CHAPTER
Seventeen

~Gabrielle~

"Wake up sleepy-head."

The bed dips down beside me, the smell of coffee wafting up into my nostrils, eliciting a low moan from me before I grumble my response. "What time is it?"

I hear cups being placed on the nightstand, then feel heaven, soft and warm brush across my lips. "It's a little after noon." His fingers sweep loose strands of my hair away from my face. "I've got to leave in a little while."

My eyes blink open, a frown pulling down my features. "Why? I thought you didn't have to work until seven." His fingers continue brushing down through my long hair, their tips grazing over the bare skin on my shoulder and arm, sending goosebumps across my skin, but in the most delicious way.

"I really want to go see Willow for a little while, and her mom said she's free this afternoon."

"Oh, okay." I wait to see if he's going to invite me to go with him. When he doesn't, I shift to a sitting position, pulling the covers up over my torso. "Are you leaving right now?" My feelings are a little hurt, even though I know I have no right to feel this way. We've known each other for less than a month, and who knows where this is going. Even though he basically told me he loved me last night.

His fingers travel back up my arm, over my shoulder and then finally skim up my face, his palm cupping my cheek. "I want to tell her about us. I'd really like the two of you to meet, but I feel like I need to at least talk to her first to get her used to the idea. Are you okay with that?"

Shit. Now I feel like an asshole for just doubting him. I really do need to learn to trust someone for once. I turn my lips into his palm and press a soft kiss to his skin. "I would love to meet your daughter."

He lifts his hand off my face, reaches for the coffee he brought me, then hands it to me. His eyes follow the cup as I bring it to my lips. "I'm going to ask you something, and I don't want you to freak out, okay?"

I lower the cup, my brow furrowing. "Okay."

He shifts his body on the bed, crosses his legs, shifts again, then looks at me. I lean over to place my coffee on the table, snapping at him. "Jesus, Cameron! Just spit it out, you're scaring me."

"I know we've only been seeing each other a short time, but I feel like I need to know this before things get any more serious." He pauses, and I nod, waving my hand for him to keep going, so he does. "Do you think you're going to want children one day?"

Not at all the question I was expecting from him. Not that I really even knew what to expect, but definitely not that. And I don't even know how to answer the damn thing. What if he doesn't want anymore kids because he already has a daughter? And if I say I do; is that the end for us? Or if I say I don't, and he does want more? I have not had enough coffee yet for this discussion. I shrug, shaking my head. "I haven't really thought about it to be honest. Why, do you?"

"I hadn't really thought about it either until last night when Charlie made a reference about it being your turn next." He scratches at his chin, his mouth frowning slightly. "And when you told her that wasn't something you had to worry about, it kind of slapped me upside the head. I don't know for sure if I want more kids in the future, but I guess I want to know the possibility is there if I do."

"This is really heavy talk first thing in the morning, Cam." I blow out a long breath.

"I know, I'm sorry." He takes my hand in his. "My timing isn't always the best."

"I can tell you this; I know that I don't not want kids. I've never had a moment where I said conclusively that I don't want children. But to be honest with you, I've never been in a serious enough relationship to have even thought about it." I take his hand into both of mine and hold it tightly. "But if there was ever anyone that would make me want to think about it, it would be you."

"Okay." He leans into me, his lips caressing mine in a soft kiss. "It's enough."

"Am I?" I wonder out loud, unsure of everything now.

His hand grips onto the back of my head, holding my forehead against his. "You're more than enough. I'm just trying to get my head to catch up with my heart."

"Don't make me fall in love with you if you're just going to break mine." I whisper.

"I promise I'm here, ready and waiting to catch you when you fall." He seals his words with a kiss, then pulls away slowly, rising from the bed. "I'll come by and pick you up tomorrow morning and take you to work, okay? Six-thirty?"

"Okay, sounds great." I blow him a kiss, then fall back on the bed, my head dizzy with emotions.

I spend another hour in bed, then force myself to get up, shower, and join the land of the living. I call Charlie to check on her and then call Faith to see how she's feeling. They discharged her from the hospital, and she's home recovering. My next call is to Cory, to try and set up a date with the senator to see if I can discover anything about Steven Bennett.

I knew what I was doing was risky, but I'd been on over a dozen dates with the senator and couldn't imagine this one would be any different than the others. Cory, although surprised, said she would reach out and check his availability. It didn't take long. She called back within an hour and said the senator would love to see me the next night. I had to work at the hospital until seven, and I knew Cameron was working the night shift, so I told her to set us up for eight o'clock.

The next morning, when Cameron picked me up for work, he looked exhausted but also happy to see me. I didn't mention my plan. I hadn't told him about my job at Temptations, nor did I plan on it if it didn't come up. That part of my life had nothing to do with his part in my life, and now that it was technically over, what would be the point?

Temptations was like Tinder for me. I just had someone else setting up the dates. And yeah, okay, so I got paid, but that was just for the date. I never once kept money that was given to me for sex. If I decided to have sex with someone, it was because it was what I wanted. So, yeah, I'm not telling him. Good decision, right?

Cameron drops me at the hospital with a kiss and a promise to pick me up again the next morning again. He's going to stay at his place on the days we work opposite shifts, so he's off to his apartment to get some sleep. The shift at the hospital flies by, and I actually get Kinsley to come in an hour early to cover for me so I can go home to get ready for dinner with the senator.

Once I'm home, I take a quick shower, blow out my hair, and look for an appropriate dress to wear in my closet. I've already decided that I'm not sleeping with the senator, or with Xander. I'm going to tell the senator that I wanted to have dinner so that I could tell him personally I was leaving Temptations, and not hear it from someone else. If he'd like me to go up to the room so he can spend some time with Xander, I'm okay with that, and actually hoping for it, so perhaps I can corner Steven.

I finally decide on something much more conservative than I would normally wear to a date. I want to make sure my message about leaving the agency is conveyed properly in all ways, including what I wear. I pick a plum colored knee-length, A-line, sleeveless, chiffon cocktail dress, with a high neck. No cleavage, no skin above the knee exposed. I pair the dress with a simple pair of black suede heels and some diamond stud earrings.

Just as I finish putting on my make-up, I receive a call letting me know my car has arrived. I pull my black fur coat out of the closet, slip it on, then dash out of my apartment. Less than thirty minutes later, I stroll into The Mark Hotel and head straight for the restaurant. It's a little after eight, so I'm not surprised that all three men are seated already and waiting for me. As I approach, all three rise in unison, greeting me, the senator pulling out a chair for me.

"Elle, you look beautiful as always." He brushes a dry kiss across my cheek as I sit.

"Thank you, Martin." I place my napkin in my lap, as I greet the other men. "Xander, Steven, so nice to see you both again."

A waiter appears at my elbow, and I order a Kettle One martini, extra dirty, extra olives. The other men already have drinks, so I ask how long they had to wait, and apologize for being late.

"So, tell me, Elle, why did you arrange dinner this evening? Cory said you had something you wanted to share with me?" The senator lifts his tumbler of scotch, I know this after all the dates we've shared, and takes a sip as he waits for my reply.

"Well, given our history and the time we've spent together, I wanted to tell you personally that I've decided to leave the agency." His brow shoots up as his tumbler thumps back to the table. I reach my hand out to place it gently over his. "I've enjoyed every moment of our time together, and cherish your friendship, but wanted this news to come from me, and not from someone else."

He leans toward me and lowers his voice. "Is it because of what happened last time we were together?" He's referring to the threesome, which really turned into a twosome between Xander and him. It was more than apparent he was at the very least bisexual, if not gay after that date.

"No!" I assure him. "Of course not." I squeeze his hand. "That doesn't matter to me one bit Martin."

The waiter appears, so we break apart, both of us sitting back while he sets the drink down in front of me. "Are you ready to order?" He inquires.

"Why don't you give us a few more minutes?" The senator shoos him away.

I grip the stem of the martini glass in my fingers and take a healthy sip, the salty burn of the alcohol warm as I swallow. I set the glass back down and make eye contact with the senator again. "If you must know, I've met someone, so this line of work just isn't appropriate for me anymore."

His face seems to relax when I explain the reason for my departure, and a second later, a warm smile tilts his lips. "Well, that's nice then Elle. I really hope you'll be happy, but I will miss you."

I lift my glass to take another sip, nodding. "We're still friends. I'm sure we'll see each other in certain circles." I take another healthy sip, preparing myself for my next comment. "I would have asked Faith to come along tonight, but she had an unfortunate incident the other day."

I keep my eyes glued to Steven so I can gauge his reaction, a small burst of electricity zapping through me when I notice his body tense, his eyes darting away from mine to avert my gaze. I continue my story, but don't look away from my target. "Yes, it seems she was attacked and beaten quite badly last week. I'm not sure when or if she'll return."

"Oh my goodness, that's awful." Martin exclaims. "You must tell me where I can send a gift to her, or flowers, please."

"I'm sure Cory at the agency could help you with that." I offer.

Xander finally speaks. "I'm going to visit her tomorrow Martin. I can bring something to her if you'd like."

Oh, this piques my interest. These two seem to have gotten much cozier since our date together. I look back and forth between them and wonder what's been happening behind the scenes that I'm not aware of. I make a mental note to give Xander a call tomorrow to get all the details.

"Nonsense, I'll have Steven take care of it." He turns his attention toward him. "That's what he's here for, right Steven?"

"Of course, Martin." Steven replies dryly, his teeth practically grating together as he does. "Should we order? I'm starving."

"Will you still stay and have dinner with us Elle?" The senator asks me.

"I'd love to, thank you." I pick up the menu, deciding quickly what I want, and set it back down. "Martin, would you order me the rib-eye medium? I'm going to use the powder room."

"Certainly." Each of the men rises slightly out of their seats when I stand, then sit again as I leave. I navigate through the dining room, and head past the bar toward the restroom. My body freezes in place when I glance at the barstools and lock onto a pair of steely grey eyes glaring straight at me.

My hand flies up to my chest as my breath catches in my throat, my mouth gaping open in silence a moment before I finally speak. "Cameron."

"Gabby." He stands, taking two steps to close the gap between us. "Or should I call you Elle?"

CHAPTER Eighteen

~Cameron~

"What are you doing here?" She stutters, her face flushed almost crimson as she stares up at me.

"Working." I wrap my hand around her bare arm and pull her further into the bar, away from any customers. "And apparently, you are too." My blood is roaring so loudly through my veins I can hear it swooshing in my ears.

Her entire body reels back at my harsh words, her eyes growing wider as she shakes her head, my hand gripping more tightly to hold her in place. "Cameron, you're hurting me."

I look down at my hand, releasing her arm immediately when I see the indents my fingers are leaving in her flesh.

"I can explain." She insists, her voice steady.

I cross my arms over my chest, squinting as I see her

through completely different eyes. "What are you going to explain that I haven't already pieced together? You're already aware that your friend, Faith, knew her alleged attacker as a client with the escort agency she works for, Temptations. Did it occur to you, that as a detective, I would reach out to that agency to determine if there were any connections to the other women that were attacked? And that I would also monitor any future dates he books with the agency? Imagine how thrilled I was when I learned he had one tonight, on a night I was actually working. I could actually observe and follow him to see if in fact, he could possibly be the perp in this case." I expel a long breath and then lean in close to her. "And imagine my surprise when *my girlfriend* arrives and sits across the table from the very man I'm supposed to be investigating, as his date. *His paid escort.*"

"I'm curious Cameron." She takes a step back from me, placing her hands on her waist. "Are you angry that I'm interfering with your investigation, or about the fact that I worked as an escort?"

"You mean, work, don't you?" I hiss back. "Because according to Temptations, one Elle Reed and Xander Walker are meeting with the senator and his associate for dinner this evening. I just never expected-" I grit my teeth and slam my hand into the wall behind her. "How the hell could you not tell me something like this? You know I work in fucking VICE, right? I arrest people like you every god damn day."

"Not like me! I am not a prostitute, Cameron!" She lifts a finger and jabs it into my chest with each word she says. "I was an escort. Legal in the state of New York. I accompanied men to dinner, to parties, sometimes to a damn funeral."

"And to their bed, if they pay you enough, right?" I seethe, my temper flaring.

Her hand rears back and slaps against my cheek in one quick stroke. "Fuck you, Cameron." She shakes her head, her eyes blazing with fury. "I am not a whore, and I will not let you make me feel like one." She plants her foot, then spins around, the skirt of her dress flying up around her as she does, then moves to stomp away.

I reach out and grab onto her arm, wrenching her back until my face is level with hers. "Where in the hell do you think you're going?"

"Back to my date." She spits out, her body jerking as she tries to break free from me.

"I don't fucking think so." I twist her arm up behind her back, a yelp sounding from her, some of the customers at the bar turning to look at us. "You're under arrest for striking an officer." I use my other hand to slide my cuffs out of my belt, click one side around her wrist, then spin her around, clicking the other one into place on her other wrist.

"Are you kidding me right now?" She stares up at me wide-eyed. "You're seriously arresting me."

"Looks like you finally got your wish babe." I grab onto the chain of the handcuffs binding her wrists together, and yank on them. "And yeah, I'm seriously arresting you." I spin her around so that her back is to my front and push her forward, through the bar, and then out into the hotel lobby. "You have the right to remain silent. You have the right to an attorney. Anything you say, can and will be used against you in a court of law. Do you understand these rights as I have explained them to you?"

"Fuck you, Cameron." She hisses over her shoulder at me. "I hate you."

Not as much as I hate myself right now.

Brian's sitting in a chair in the entryway, and jumps up when he sees me coming, a look of confusion on his face. "What are you doing?"

"Making an arrest. You got a problem with that?" I bite out.

He lifts his hands in the air, as he backs up. "Nope."

"Good." I stop, my grip firm around Gabby's arm. "Inform the rest of the party in there that their *date* had to leave. Keep an eye on our suspect for us. I'll be back."

His eyes bounce from me to Gabby, then back to me before he nods. "Okay."

"Let's go." I push her forward again, heading toward the exit.

"Can I at least get my coat? It's thirty degrees outside." She glares at me over her shoulder.

I halt. "Where is it?"

"Coat check."

Luckily it's directly to our left, so I veer that way, stepping up to the booth. The attendant looks at the handcuffs around Gabby's wrists, then up at me, not sure who to address. "Can you get her jacket?"

"Does she have a claim ticket?" She replies nervously.

"Jesus Christ. I just gave it to you twenty minutes ago. A black, fur coat." Gabby barks to the attendant.

"Okay, yes, you're right. Sorry." She holds a finger up as she turns. "One minute." She's back in less than that, the fur draped over her arm, which she sets on the counter between us. "Here."

Gabby lets out a sigh. "I can't exactly put it on with these damn things on." She rattles the metal around her wrists.

"Fine." I huff, grabbing the coat off the counter. I arrange it so it falls over her shoulders, refusing to take the cuffs off now out of spite. I lead her out of the hotel, and over to the curb where my car is parked. I open the back and motion for her to get in.

She looks up at me, eyes wide as she shakes her head in disbelief. "You're making me sit in the back?"

"Just get in Gabby." I give her a small shove, making it clear I'm not fooling around.

"You're such a god damn bastard." She mutters as she drops down into the seat and I slam the door.

I walk around the back of the car, stopping when I'm behind it, and stomp my foot in anger. "Fuck!" If I had hair right now, I'd be gripping onto it and ripping it from my head. How the hell did I get here with her? Yesterday we were lying in bed together, and now she's in the back of my damn squad car. I look up at the night sky, and seeing only blackness, close my eyes to let out a long breath. *Worse fucking night ever*. I blow out one more breath, then continue around the car to climb in the driver's seat.

Neither one of us says anything as I pull into traffic and start driving uptown. After several moments of silence, I can't take it anymore and speak. "How long Gabby?"

"How long what?" Her voice comes from behind me.

"How long have you been an escort?"

"Nine months or so. But I'm not anymore. I quit. As soon as I slept with you, I knew I couldn't do it anymore."

"Lucky me." I scoff.

"Don't be such an asshole."

"I guess I should be happy at the discovery that my girlfriend is an escort?"

"I *was* an escort, Cameron. You seem to be missing the part where I told you I quit."

"How many men Gabby? How many of the *dates* you escorted did you sleep with?" My fingers tighten around the steering wheel as I wait for her response.

"How many of the dates have you slept with, that you went out with over the last few years Cameron? Why don't you answer that?"

"Because I wasn't hired to take anyone out. It's completely different."

"Not really. You pay one way or the other. A hundred bucks for dinner, fifty bucks for the movies, seventy-five for drinks and appetizers at the bar. Maybe you get laid, maybe you don't. But don't try to fool yourself into thinking you didn't go out on any of those dates with the intention of not getting laid."

"And can the same be said about you and your dates?" I shoot back, angry that she's not off base.

"If I liked someone I went on a date with, and I wanted to sleep with him, then I did. I like sex. I'm not ashamed to admit that Cameron. But don't make me feel cheap for it. I never asked, nor did I ever take money from anyone for sex. It was always consensual and it was always safe."

I don't say anything else. Mostly because I don't want to know any more than I already do, and also because I know some of what she's saying is true. I pull the car out of traffic and park next to the curb, turning around in my seat.

"What the fuck were you doing at that hotel then, with those men, if you aren't an escort anymore?"

"I wanted to see if it was Steven that hurt Faith. So, I had the agency set up the dinner. I told the Senator that I had left the agency, but wanted to tell him myself. It was dinner, that's it."

"How the hell did you think you were going to help Faith by having dinner with this monster?"

She leans forward in the seat. "I brought up Faith. I mentioned she had been attacked. You should have seen how he reacted. I know it was him."

"God damn it, Gabby!" I roar angrily. "Are you trying to get yourself killed? If he suspects you are on to him, he'll hurt you next. This isn't a fucking game."

"But I know he did it. I could tell by the-"

"Just stop." I slam my hand against the seat between us, her body flinching back. "Just let me do my damn job, and keep your nose out of it. You've done enough damage."

"I just wanted to help Faith." She mutters.

"You didn't." I turn back around and pull the car back into traffic. We're silent the rest of the trip until I pull into the drive, and get out of the car. I hold my hand out to stop the valet and open the back door myself.

"What are you doing?" She asks quietly, looking up at me.

I fish a set of keys out of my pocket and point to her hands. "Let me see your wrists."

She lifts them, and I turn the key in each cuff, releasing them from her, then fold them back into my belt. "Go home Gabby." I step back so she can get out of the car.

She slides off the seat and stands next to me. "You're not arresting me?"

I glance at her, then glance away, her eyes too hard to look at right now. "Stay away from Bennett and the senator."

She takes a step toward me, but I counter and step back. If she touches me, I'll lose it.

"Cameron." She reaches out for me, but I turn and walk back around the car to the driver's side.

"I can't do this Gabby." I look up, meet her eyes for just a second, then shake my head. "I'm sorry." I climb into the car, slam the door, and drive away, making sure I don't look in the rearview mirror to see the tears falling from her face again.

CHAPTER Nineteen

~Gabrielle~

I call into work the next day because my eyes are so swollen from crying that I can barely open them. And also, because I know that even if I did go in, I would be useless. I feel like I've been run over by a truck, or at least my insides do. Feeling like this is the one reason I never wanted to fall in love. I've seen too many of my friends in the exact same position I am now.

Xander came by earlier this morning to drop off my purse and phone, which were left behind on the table when Cameron *arrested* me. He wanted details, but I just didn't have the energy to try and explain my fucked-up love life. And as much as I wanted to find out what was going on with him and the senator, it would have to wait for another day. After Xander left, I crawled back into bed, bury myself under covers smothered in Cameron's scent, and cry myself back to sleep.

I wake up a little after seven, and the first thing I do is grab my phone to see if he tried to call or text me. He didn't. My heart sinks even deeper into the pit of despair that was previously known as my stomach. There's a small part of me, okay, maybe it was more than a small part, that hoped he might have shown up here before his shift tonight.

I stare down at my phone, my fingers hovering over the keyboard, as I wage a silent war with myself about whether or not to text him. Do I want to be *that* girl? You know the one I mean; desperate and needy. Because that's *never* been me. I've always been the girl that walks away without looking back, and without a single ounce of regret or remorse for doing so. But god help me, I've also never been a girl in love. Nope, not going to go there. I toss my phone away from me onto the other side of the bed. I throw the covers off of me and stomp to my bathroom, yank open the drawer containing all my medicine and paw through it until I find what I'm looking for. I pop the cap off the bottle, shake two Xanax into my palm, leave the rest of the container on the counter, shove the pills in my mouth and then go climb back into my bed.

I sleep ten blissful hours, crawling slowly back to consciousness when the sun streaks through the blinds I neglected to close yesterday. My lips actually start to curve up into a smile for all of three seconds; the exact amount of time it takes for reality to come crashing back as Cameron's face flashes through my mind. I sit up and sift around in the comforter trying to locate my phone, grabbing on to and waving it triumphantly in the air when I find it. I swipe up to see if I have any missed calls or texts, and growl, slamming the phone back onto the bed when all I get is a blank screen. Fricking phone is dead.

I roll out of the bed, the phone clutched tightly in my hand, and walk over to my dresser, plugging it into the charger. I leave it, knowing if I stand there waiting for it to power back on will be like waiting for water to boil, and head to the bathroom instead. I use the toilet, splash some water over my face, and brush my teeth. By the time I get back to my dresser, I hear my phone buzz to life, my pulse kicking up a notch as I lift the phone and swipe again. I have three messages!

I go to voicemail to look at the messages, my heart sinking when none are Cameron's number. Two are from Charlie and one is the hospital number. I slam the phone back down on the dresser and scream out my frustration. "Fuck you too Cameron!" I'm not going to let myself sit here and wallow any longer, so I pull out a pair of clean scrubs and underwear while I'm at my dresser, then drag myself back to the bathroom for a shower.

Work the next two days absolutely sucks. I'm a complete bitch to every single person I encounter, patients and coworkers alike, my patience non-existent. I think everyone was relieved when I finally left today, no one more so than myself. I still hadn't received a single call or text from Cameron. I was off the next three days and had no idea how the hell to fill my time now that I no longer seemed to have him or Temptations in my life. I stop at a liquor store on my way home and grab a jumbo bottle of white wine figuring I might as well try to drown my sorrows.

Three hours later, three-quarters of the way into the bottle, and half-way through Pretty Woman, I do what every heartbroken, intoxicated person is not supposed to do and start drunk texting. And not just once. Oh no, if I was going to do this, I was going all in.

10:15 PM Outgoing Text to Hot Detective (I never did get around to updating his contact information in my phone)

~You said you would catch me when I fell. Why am I here all alone then?

11:03 PM Outgoing Text to Hot Detective

~She was right. Only Cinder-fucking-rella gets the happily ever after

11:38 PM Outgoing Text to Hot Detective

~Don't you miss me at all? How can you just ignore me?

12:47 AM Outgoing Text to Hot Detective

~My bed feels empty without you in it

1:03 AM Outgoing Text to Hot Detective

~I hate you for this you fucking coward

I jerk awake, my eyes snapping open, my head exploding in pain. "Oooh." I rub my temple with my fingers, then freeze when I hear loud knocking on my door. *That's why I woke up.* I stumble out of my bed, tripping over my own feet when I finally land on them, almost falling on my face. I catch myself on the bed, stand up straight, then scamper to the door when someone knocks again. When I reach the door, I yank it open, only to falter back two steps when I realize who it is.

"We need to talk."

Jesus, did he always look that good in a suit, or is it because I haven't seen him in four days. I stare at him, my mouth hanging slightly open, my brain too hungover or surprised to form any words.

"Can I come in?" He's glaring at me, the tone of his voice hard. The brief moment of euphoria I felt upon seeing him gone. *Guess this isn't a booty call.*

"Sure." I let go of the door as I turn away, then begin walking toward the living room. I feel like I'm going to puke, my stomach tossing and turning as I lower myself onto one of the couches, looking up at him, his posture rigid as he crosses his arms. I jolt up off the couch. "Do you want a cup of coffee?"

"I don't want a fucking cup of coffee, Gabby." He shifts, widening his stance. "You tell me you miss me, then tell me you hate me, then call me a fucking coward. The texts need to stop. I thought giving you a clean break would make this easier, but if you need me to tell you it's over in person, so you have closure, here I am."

Several thoughts race through my mind at once; *shit, the fucking texts!, how many did I end up sending??, and what about any of this is easy?* I lower my body slowly back onto the couch again, a shaky breath leaving me as I lift my eyes to his. "You think I need closure?"

"I'm not sure what you need, but I thought I made it clear the other night that this is over."

I drag my eyes down his frame, pausing briefly on the gun holstered at his waist until I reach his feet. I try to rationalize what's coming out of the person's mouth standing before me, compared to the one that held me in his arms less than a week ago. "Are you really that cold?" I tilt my head as I look back up at his face.

He uncrosses his arms, lifting one hand to drag roughly

over his head as he heaves a loud sigh. "You lied to me Gabby. About who you are, what you did, the kind of person you are. You broke my damn heart."

"I broke your heart?" I bolt upright, my voice raising. "You put handcuffs on me! You arrested me and dragged me out of a hotel. You dropped me off after barely having a conversation about it, on the curb like a god damn hooker at that, and then cut me out of your life like I meant nothing to you!" I scoff, waving my hands in front of me. "After telling me that you love me! You don't treat people you love this way!"

He takes two large strides toward me then stops, his nostrils flaring as deep breaths sound from them. "I don't even know who you are Gabby!"

"How can you even say that?" I wrap my arms around myself, my hands clenching into fists as I try to maintain some of my composure as I feel my heart crumble in on itself. "I'm the girl whose hair smells like coconut, who doesn't wear makeup to work, and who you thought liked wearing scrubs but really would prefer to be naked. I like tequila, pretty dresses, and feeling your hand in mine. And you were right when I said I wanted everyone to think I was happy living in this fancy hotel. I didn't know how wrong I was until I woke up here with you in my arms and realized what true happiness was. And look," I shrug my shoulders and hold my hands up, still clenched. "I don't know if I should be really angry at you for thinking my being an escort defines who I am, or really scared that everything you said you felt for me, just doesn't matter anymore."

He stares at me, blinking several times as the very words he said to me weeks ago are used against him. When he finally speaks, his voice is low and calm. "I did care about you." He closes his eyes, turning his head to the ceiling for a moment before looking at me again. "I do care about you."

I take a step closer to him, tentatively reaching my hand out to his, my breath catching when he steps back abruptly. That one action speaks volumes, my veins turning to ice as my blood runs cold, hurt and anger seething as I point toward the door. "Get out."

He flinches as though I slapped him, his mouth opening to say something, stopping when I step to shove him hard with both hands. "Go!"

His eyes go wide as he stumbles sideways. "Jesus, Gabby! Let me say something." He argues as he rights himself.

I shake my head, angry at myself as I feel tears start to well. "You've said enough." I point to the door again. "Just leave."

He nods once, then spins on his heel, marching out of the living room and out my door, the sound of the latch clicking behind him, triggering me to crumple to my knees as I break down crying.

I don't know how long I've been on the floor. Long enough that there isn't a single tear left for me to cry. Long enough for me to come to the conclusion that wine or Xanax isn't going to help me this time. I decide the only way I'm going to feel better is to find a way to forget about Cameron Justice. And what better way to do that, than to find another man to distract me. Luckily for me, I know just the man to help me.

I start drinking before I even get in the shower, opening a new bottle of Patron to throw back a shot. I do another shot when I'm out of the shower, and then another when I'm putting on my makeup. The fact that I haven't eaten in over a day catches up to me on the ride across town, my thoughts starting to get nice and fuzzy as the driver drops me off. I stride into the building, no one even blinking or questioning the fact that I'm carrying an open bottle of tequila as I board the elevator. They know me here, obviously.

I press the number eight, and on the way up, pop the cork off the bottle and take another swig for courage. When I get to his door, I don't bother knocking, knowing he rarely locks his door, and just turn the knob to enter his apartment, trying to work in the element of surprise.

Well, fuck, guess the surprise is on me. That sexy little brunette from the ball is standing in his living room. I place my hand on my hip and swing it out for effect. "Well, what do we have here?"

The woman's eyes squint, her cheeks flaming red as she squares her body off against mine. "Trick's out, but he should be back in just a minute. Can I help you with something?"

Not unless you have a dick, honey. That's what I want to say, but before I can, I see Trick storming down the hall. "I'm a friend of Tricks. I was just stopping by-" I swing my head briefly in his direction. "Oh look, here he is now." I graze my fingers over Trick's arm when he walks past me into the room. "Loverboy is back."

I watch as he puts down a puppy, (*when in the hell did he get a puppy*), and then places a bag on the counter, his face angry when he turns back to me. "What the fuck are you doing here, Gabby?"

I saunter a few feet into the apartment. "Charlie told me

you'd been down in the dumps lately, so I thought I'd come by and cheer you up." I hold up the bottle of tequila, then turn my head toward the brunette, arching my brow as I add a heavy dose of sarcasm. "But looks like someone already beat me to it."

The feisty brunette plants her hands on her hips and glares at me but is absolutely addressing Trick. "I thought you said you were just friends with her."

Trick steps between us. "We are just friends. She has a damn boyfriend." He turns his attention to me, pointing a finger at the other woman. "Tell her."

I shrug nonchalantly because right now, fuck everyone. "I tried. She didn't believe me. Maybe because we've fucked before she thinks we can't be friends."

Before I can blink, Trick's hand is clasped around my arm. "What the fuck is wrong with you?" He rears back, his nostrils flaring. "And why are you drunk at six o'clock?"

"Don't touch me!" I wrench my arm out of his grasp, pulling so hard that I lose my balance in the four-inch heels I'm wearing, and have to grab onto his shoulder so I won't fall. I steady myself then make a dramatic turn toward the door. "I'm leaving."

"Where the hell do you think you're going?" He grabs onto my arm again, following me into the hallway. I mutter more profanities at him, raking my nails across his hand when he won't let go.

He scoffs. "That won't work on me Gabby I like the pain, remember?" He tugs me against him, lowering his voice in concern. "What the hell is going on with you?"

Fuck him for caring. This isn't what I need from him. I don't need him to be my therapist. Instead of telling him, I turn even nastier. "Sorry if I ruined your date." I glance over my shoulder through the open door. "Looks like you got to fuck her already though, so not all's lost. Does she know how much you like-"

"Enough!" He roars, just as the elevator doors slide open, Charlie stepping out. *Great, can this party get any more fun?* He shoves me toward my friend, releasing my arm. "Take her before I do something I regret."

Charlie catches me in her arms, wrapping one around my waist, shooting Trick a confused look.

"She's drunk. Something's wrong. But instead of telling me, she went into full on bitch mode."

"Yeah, I love you too, Trick." I taunt over my shoulder as Charlie drags me into the elevator.

"Stop it, Gabrielle!" Charlie admonishes, then wraps her arms around me in a hug. "What's wrong?"

I drop my head onto her shoulder, my body beginning to shake as I lean into her. I spend the next couple of hours crying on her shoulder as I tell her everything. Believe it or not, I feel better after sharing it with her. She just listened to me, no judgment, no blame, and no more tequila, which I'm sure also helped matters. She tries to get me to spend the night, but her couch is the last place I want to be. Even if it's painful, I'd rather go home and curl under covers that smell like Cameron, savoring that small little piece of him I still have left.

CHAPTER Twenty

~Cameron~

I pull into the line of parents waiting to pick up kids in front of Willow's school and put the car in park. I get out, go around to the trunk, then pop it open to grab the booster seat I keep there for her. I open the back door, then arrange it in the seat. I lean against the car as I wait for her, my face pulling up into the first smile I've had in days, as she skips towards me, her braids bouncing on her head.

"Daddy!" She jumps into my outstretched arms, throwing her hands around my neck to hug me as I lift her.

"How's my little bean?" I squeeze her back, needing this hug more than she can know.

"I'm good." She pulls back, moving her face so it's in front of mine. "Are we still going to Auntie Adaline's?"

"We sure are." I lower her into the back seat, buckle her in, then drop a kiss on the tip of her nose. "You excited to see your cousin?"

"Yes!" She exclaims, clapping her hands. "Can I sleep over daddy? Please?"

I chuckle at her excitement. Adaline is the younger of my two older sisters, and also has a daughter, Jada, who's just a little older than Willow. "We'll see baby, okay?" I shut the door and climb into the driver's seat, trying to hurry before the mom behind me starts honking.

The radio squawks as I pull into traffic, and I reach out to turn it off. I don't like Willow hearing some of the things that come across it, and I'm off duty until Tuesday. If someone needs me, they'll call me. It takes us a good forty-five minutes to get into Brooklyn where Adaline lives, but the ride flies by as Willow tells me about her week at school and about her upcoming dance recital. At this current moment in time, it's Willow's dream to become a premier ballerina in the New York City Ballet, so her world consists of tights, tutus, and twirling. I love hearing about every minute of it because as soon as we walk into Adaline's house, I am completely forgotten and replaced by Jada.

"Hey, baby brother!" Adaline greets me as I enter the kitchen. "I thought I heard the happy screeching of six-year-old girls." She giggles as she hugs me. "You want something to drink?"

"I'd love a beer if you have one." I drop a kiss on top of her head, then move to sit at the table.

"Dave always has a few in the fridge." She opens the door and peers inside. "He's got Blue Moon or Budweiser."

"I'll take a Bud." She snatches a bottle off the shelf, then turns to hand it to me. "Thanks."

"You gonna stay for dinner?" She pulls a large, square container out of the fridge. "I'm making chicken."

"Is that mom's recipe? The tangy flavored one?" I arch a brow, eyeing the container.

"It sure is." She sets it on the counter. "And I'm making mashed potatoes and green beans too."

"Then hell yes, I'm staying for dinner." I take a drink of my beer, smiling around the bottle.

Four hours later, after an amazing dinner, and agreeing to let Willow spend the night with her cousin, I trudge back out to my car to head back into the city. I could have just hopped on I-278 and been back in Harlem in thirty minutes, but instead, I opt for the FDR and head back into downtown.

I'm exhausted. After I left Gabby's this morning, it took me four hours to fall asleep, the alarm going off three hours after that to pick Willow up from school. I hate how I left things this morning with Gabby. I was a prick. I'm mad at her for all the wrong reasons, and only punishing us both by staying away from her. Every single thing she said to me was true. I am in love with her. The discovery that she was an escort, doesn't change that fact.

I'm pissed that she just didn't tell me about it to begin with. Pissed that she could have told me when Faith was brought into the hospital. Or after. Or before she decided to put herself in harm's way by having dinner with the monster that might be responsible for not only Faith but numerous other women who have been beaten. And I'm pissed that I acted like such a shallow asshole when I found out. My reaction only solidified all the reasons she probably thought she couldn't tell me.

The truth of the matter is, what she did before me, doesn't even matter. Any more than what I did in my past before I met her matters. She certainly didn't hold my failed marriage against me or the fact that I have a child. Even after I told her the marriage failed because my drive for my career was more important to me than my own wife. She still trusted in the person I was now, not who I was before. What a hypocrite I was that I couldn't afford her the same benefit of the doubt.

So, here I am, on the FDR, hoping that she'll open the door to listen to me grovel for forgiveness and another chance to prove myself. Five days without her was five more than I ever wanted to spend away from her again. If I hadn't been such a stubborn asshole when I was at her place this morning, I could have admitted that. Now I had to hope she wasn't so angry that she couldn't forgive me.

It's just after nine-thirty when I approach The Pierre. I frown when I see the flashing lights of an ambulance and squad car across the street at the park entrance. I let out a sigh of relief and say a small prayer of thanks that I'm not on duty to have to deal with whatever it is. The valet actually recognizes me, and waves me toward a spot just past the hotel entrance, running to open my door once I'm parked.

"You staying the night, detective, or should I keep it here?" He adjusts his cap as he stands beside the car.

"You know, I'm honestly not sure." I hand him the keys. "If I'm not back in an hour, why don't you park it for the night."

"Yes, sir." He pockets the keys and nods.

"Thanks." I stride past him to make my way into the building, then to the elevator, and up to the twelfth floor. I'm not going to lie, my heart is banging against my chest as I approach her door, more nervous to knock than I am interrogating known murderers. I draw in a ragged breath, blow it out, and rap my knuckles against the wood. I wait, shuffling my feet back and forth, silence the only reply. I knock again, a little louder this time in case she's sleeping. After another minute and no answer, I pull my cell out and try to call. It goes straight to voicemail, my lips grimacing in frustration. *Where the hell is she?* I hit end without leaving a message. I knock one more time, just to be sure, but after waiting, and still no answer, I give up and make my way out of the hotel.

"No luck?" The valet jogs up to me, my keys in his outstretched hand.

"Nope." I look him in the eye. "Did you see Miss Reed go out tonight?"

"No, sir." He swipes his hand across his nose. "But I just came on duty at nine."

"Okay." I start to walk away, then turn back. "If you happen to see her come in later, will you tell her I stopped by?"

"Yeah, sure. No problem."

I give him a nod of thanks, then climb in my car to head home, my stomach in knots, a feeling of defeat haunting me. When I get home, I try Gabby's phone one more time, voicemail picking up immediately again. Maybe she turned her phone off? This time I do leave a message, asking her to please call me, and hope like hell when she hears it, she will. I strip out of my clothes, crawl under my blankets, and succumb to exhaustion, falling asleep almost instantly.

"What?" I sit straight up, jerking awake. My phone vibrates on the stand next to my bed, and I realize it must have woken me up. I snatch it up, blinking my eyes into focus to see the caller id.

"Brian, what's up?" I grumble roughly, not quite awake yet.

"Christ, man, I've been trying to call you for over an hour."

"I was asleep." I glance over at the clock to see what time it is. "Why are you calling me at seven-fucking-thirty on my day off?"

"You need to get down to University Hospital Cam. Now." A heavy sigh sounds on the other end of the phone. "It's Gabby. She was brought in last night."

My legs fly out of the bed and land on the floor as I jump up. "What do you mean she was brought in?" Adrenaline shoots through my system, the hairs across my body prickling as my voice rises.

"She was found just inside the entrance to the park last night, right after nine." He lets out another breath. "It's pretty bad Cameron. She still hasn't regained consciousness."

"What?" I bark, my heart literally stopping in my chest, as I fall back, my ass landing hard on my bed, as I try to catch my breath.

"Cam, just get down here, okay?"

I nod, my mind flooding with the memory of the red lights I saw across the street from her hotel last night when I arrived. Holy shit. I was right there. She was right there.

"Cameron!" Brian yells into the phone.

"Yeah, yeah. I'm here." I drag my hand down my face. "I'm coming."

CHAPTER
Twenty-One

~Gabrielle~

I step out of the Uber Charlie called for me and head inside the hotel, the desire to lose myself in sleep overwhelming. I press the call button for the elevator, my phone buzzing inside my purse at the same time. I retrieve it, swiping to read the new text.

8:38 PM Incoming Text from Xander Walker

~Can you meet me at The Plaza for a drink? The Oak Room? Need to talk.

Ugh. The last thing I want to do is hear about someone else's love life, but dammit, Xander wouldn't text me unless he really needed a friend. I type back a quick text.

8:40 PM Outgoing Text to Xander Walker

~Sure, be there in ten.

The only saving grace is that The Plaza is a short walk away, just across the street diagonally from my hotel, so at least I don't have to arrange for another ride. I turn around to head back in the direction I just came from, tugging my coat a little tighter around myself when a gust of wind blows down the street I'm crossing. I'm surprised that I'm the only one in the cross-walk as I make way across Fifth Avenue and onto the sidewalk in front of the park. It's usually quite busy still this time of night, but perhaps the cooler temperature has people inside.

"Help me." I stop in my tracks, not sure if I heard what I thought I just heard, and cock my head to listen. "Please, help me." A soft voice pleads from the direction of the park entrance. Without even thinking, I turn toward the cobbled path that leads to a stairwell into the park and call out as I step forward. "Hello? Is someone there?"

I glance up at the street lamp that should be working, uttering a curse under my breath at the City of New York for not doing a better job at replacing broken or worn out bulbs. I fish my phone out of my pocket and swipe it open to find the flashlight application, pressing on the icon to try and illuminate the path in front of me. I call out again. "Hello?"

"Please, help me." The voice pleads again. I take another step, but then freeze, some common-sense filtering through my concern, and bring my phone up again. I hit 9-1-1, then lift the phone to my ear as I continue down the path. The operator answers at the exact same time a hand wraps around my head, slamming over my mouth, another hand latching onto my neck, squeezing as I'm yanked toward the stairs.

I drop my phone to claw at the grip closing off my airway, trying to scream around the hand on my mouth, all my actions thwarted when my attacker slams my head into the stone wall. "Shut the fuck up you bitch or I'll kill you."

Hot breath spits onto my face as it's yanked back from the wall, a warm trickle of fluid running into my eyes as they lock onto wild eyes gleaming back at me through a mask covered face.

I blink, black dots swirling in my vision, my knees scraping over the rough stones as the man literally drags me down the steps by my neck, my body twisting under me as I try to get my feet under me. I cry out for help, my voice ragged from being choked, and he stops. "I said to shut the fuck up." His knee jerks up and drives up into my ribs, the wind knocked from my lungs at the impact, my body keeling over in pain.

His hand on my mouth releases to fist in my hair as he continues his descent down the stairs, my body now bouncing off each step he hauls me down. It's actually a relief when my body thumps against the ground at the bottom, the sharp edges of the stone steps no longer ripping away my skin. "Please, stop." I beg, holding my hands up in front of my face as he releases me.

I'm rewarded with another kick in the stomach, followed by a punch to my face. "Shut the fuck up, you god damn whore." My head rocks back against the pavement, a loud thud echoing inside my skull at the contact, my tongue caught between my teeth as my jaw snaps shut, blood pouring down my throat.

"Couldn't leave well enough alone, could you?" Another hard kick to my stomach, my body trying to curl in on itself in protection as I whimper. "Thought you were smart getting the police involved, you fucking cunt." His foot slams into my crotch, a scream gurgling from my throat. He bends down beside my head, his hand in my hair again, fisting it as he yanks my head off the ground, bringing it within inches of his face. "I thought I told you to shut the fuck up." Then he shoves my head back into the pavement, slamming it hard, my world going black.

Two Days Later

Why won't that damn beeping stop? My head hurts. Did I finish that bottle of tequila? I moan, my mouth feeling like it's stuffed with cotton, I try to lift my hand, but it's so heavy. I try to blink my eyes open, but they seemed to be glued shut.

"Gabby?" I feel warmth wrap around my fingers and Charlie's familiar voice. "Sweetie, can you open your eyes?"

I try again to pry my eyes open, the light blinding me when they finally crack, water immediately pooling in them, my head rearing back as I scrunch them closed again. "Too bright." I mumble, trying to lift a hand again to shield my eyes.

"Trey, shut the lights off." Charlie commands, the switch clicking, dimming the brightness on the other side of my lids. "And go get Cameron, please." Fingers squeeze my hand gently as her voice sounds next to my ear again. "Try to open your eyes again Gabby."

I concentrate on my lids, trying to ignore the hammer banging inside my head, and force them to open, blinking several times to try and focus.

"There you are." Charlie's face in front of mine, a relieved smile on her face as tears stream down her cheeks.

"Why are you crying?" I croak, my throat dry and sore as I speak.

She shakes her head as she wipes her cheeks. "Gabby, you're at the hospital. Do you remember what happened to you?"

As soon as she asks me the question, my memory comes flooding back, a deep moan wailing up from my chest as my body begins to shake uncontrollably, my head bobbing up and down, my mouth opening wide. Her arms slide around me, her belly pressing into me as she holds onto me, her breath warm against my ear as she whispers. "It's okay. You're safe. We've got you now. You're safe sweetie."

I rock against her and sob, every muscle in my body screaming in pain as each breath leaves my body in heaving gasps, her warmth never leaving me. The door behind her wrenches open, and I flinch back into the bed out of her arms, cowering away from the motion. My heart lurches in my chest when my eyes land on the tall form silhouetted darkly in the doorway. "Cameron?"

In two long strides, he's beside the bed, his arms sliding delicately around my back before pulling me ever so gently against the large, warm expanse of his chest. "You're awake." His lips press to my head as he holds me. "Thank god. I was so scared Gabby." More kisses. "I'm so sorry. I should have been there." His arms tightening ever so slightly around me, my brain fuzzy and dazed as it tries to digest everything he's mumbling. "I love you so much."

I melt into his embrace, his arms around me providing a cocoon of protection I'm craving right now, his words drifting into my consciousness, a warmth spreading over me, relieving the chill that was wracking my body. "Are you really here?"

"I'm here." His deep voice vibrates against my ear. "Where I should have always been." He leans back to look at me. "I'm so sorry, Gabby." His voice cracks, his eyes snapping closed as he shakes his head.

"This isn't your fault." I whisper, knowing without a doubt whose it is. "Where is he? Please tell me he's been arrested."

Cameron nods. "He's not a problem anymore." He pulls me into his arms again. "He'll never hurt anyone again."

Relief surges through me, but also concern. "What did you do Cameron?"

"Shhh." His hand massages a small circle on my back. "Don't worry about that." He lowers me back against my pillow. "Just rest."

It's like a spell has been cast the moment he says those words, an overwhelming urge to close my eyes washing over me, my lids so heavy I can barely keep them open. "Don't leave me."

"I won't." He bends, his lips pressing against my forehead. "Just sleep. I'll be right here."

When I wake again, all sense of time is lost to me, Cameron's in a chair next to the bed, his head lying next to my waist, my hand in his, as light snores leave him. I don't want to wake him, but I'm so thirsty. My throat feels like someone dumped a bucket of sand down it, the granules grinding against one another every time I swallow. I clench my fingers, squeezing his, and drag out his name. "Cameron."

He jerks up, his head snapping up off the bed, his eyes flying to mine. "Gabby?" He scoots closer to me. "Are you okay?"

"Thirsty." I rasp out.

"Here." He twists around, grabs a cup off the table behind him, then moves it under my mouth, a straw sliding between my lips. I inhale, the liquid so cool and sweet as it bursts through the opening and onto my tongue. I hum gratefully, my eyes closing at the delicious relief the water brings me. When I'm done, I release the straw and sit back. "Thank you."

He nods, placing the cup back down behind him. "Of course." He takes my hand in his again. "How are you? Are you in pain?"

I nod. "How long have I been asleep?"

"It's Monday afternoon."

Holy shit. I've been here for almost three days. "How bad am I hurt?"

His eyes shift away from me for only a split second, and I know instantaneously that it can't be good. "Everything will heal. It's just going to take a little time. They had to remove your spleen and part of your liver."

"What?" I wrench my fingers out of his and move them to lower the covers, then raise my dressing gown to expose my waist. "I had surgery?" My fingers tremble as they trace over the bandage on my waist, and then around the edges where dark blue and purple bruises cover my stomach. Tears start falling from my eyes as I look up at him questioningly. "What else?"

He frowns, a sigh leaving him. "Your skull is fractured,

and you needed eleven stitches to close a gash on the back of your head."

My hand flies to the back of my head, and I gasp when I feel my bare scalp and a bandage where my hair should be. I shake my head, tears falling even harder now as I blink through them to look at him again. "What else?"

"Your legs were badly cut and scraped. There are several places you needed to be stitched, and your cheekbone has a hairline fracture in it." His voice cracks and he clears his throat.

My head just shakes back and forth, the enormity of my injuries sinking in, the reason I'm in so much pain more obvious now. Cameron strokes a single finger across my cheeks, as soft as a feather, wiping the tears away. "Everything will heal, Gabby."

I scoff, more tears falling. "Will it?"

CHAPTER
Twenty~Two

~Cameron~

It's been a little over two weeks since Gabby was discharged from the hospital, and while her external wounds are visibly healing, internally we still have a mountain to climb. She spent the first ten days after leaving the hospital at her parent's house in Bridgeport, over an hour away from the city. While I understood her desire to be home, where she felt the safest, and in a place where she had people constantly available to care for her, I didn't like being so far away from her.

I called in favors and had my shifts covered by other people in the precinct, and went to see her every single day but one. On that day, I was with Willow, who had been short-changed in the worst of ways while I tried to care for Gabby. I was lucky in the fact that Willow's mom understood my situation, and had the grace to let me do what I needed without making me feel awful for neglecting our daughter. I was fortunate in more ways than one, and I recognized that, especially after realizing what I could have lost after Gabby's attack.

When Gabby finally felt well enough to go back to her apartment in the city, it was me who brought her. Me who stayed with her every single night, holding her when she woke up screaming in fear, promising her she was safe. And me who cooked for her, helped her bathe and took her to see the counselor that Trick's girlfriend, Annabelle, recommended.

But even through all that, it was also me that felt I couldn't do enough to make up for the fact that I wasn't there when I should have been. Surprisingly, Gabby was dealing with the aftermath of the assault better than I seemed to be. I was drowning in the guilt that my behavior, my stubbornness, my stupidity over her past may have directly impacted and caused her to be attacked. And I couldn't help but wonder, if there was a part of her that also felt the same, and blamed me for what happened to her. Until I had a better understanding of where we stood, how she felt, and what she wanted, I would continue to be here for her. Even if it meant sleeping on her couch to make sure she was safe or needed me to hold her in the middle of the night when she woke up screaming in fear. She holds all the cards now, and I won't push her. When she was ready, and when she invited me, I would happily return to her bed and heart.

I worked at the precinct for a few hours this afternoon, and was now headed back to Gabby's apartment to make her dinner, and spend another night on the couch watching over her. I'm surprised when I enter the apartment and hear music streaming over the speakers and noise coming from the kitchen. I shut the door behind me, then stroll through the living room towards the sound of the clattering going on. I stop, cocking my head, as I take in Gabby, a hammer hovering just over a wine bottle she's grasping in her hand.

"What in the world are you doing?" I chuckle.

She jumps a mile, and I curse internally for sneaking up on her, but she turns, a smile on her face. "I want a glass of wine but I can't get the damn cork out."

"So, you were going to just do what?" I walk into the kitchen and snag the hammer out of her hand. "Smash the top off?"

"No." She places a fist on her hip. "I was going to try and pound the cork through the bottle, using that knife to push it through." She points to a butter knife on the counter.

"Well, I'll give you points for being creative, but I don't think that would have worked out very well for you, princess." I pull the wine opener out of the drawer and begin turning it in the cork.

"Thank you." She says softly.

I look over as I pop the cork and smile. "You're welcome."

"Not for the wine, Cameron." She shakes her head, placing a hand over my arm as I set the bottle down. "For everything else. I haven't said that to you yet."

One side of my mouth turns down in a frown as I swing my eyes up to meet hers. "And I haven't said I'm sorry."

"For what?" Her head tilts, her brows furrowing.

"For everything." I tear my gaze away from her eyes, the skin around them still a dull yellow from the bruising, and look down at my feet. "For reacting the way I did when I found out about your job at Temptations. For putting handcuffs on you like you were a criminal. For pushing you away. For lying to you about the way I felt." I blow out a breath and look up at the ceiling, finally saying to her what I've been thinking for weeks. "Maybe if I had been a better man, a bigger man, and not let my pride get in the way, none of this would have happened to you."

She grabs my face in her hands and yanks it down to hers. "Cameron, what happened to me was not your fault. Steven Bennett is a fucking psycho. He would have found a way to get to me one way or another." She releases her grip but keeps her face in mine. "You do not get to be the victim here." She shakes her head angrily. "This happened to me." She points to herself. "Me." Then shakes her head again. "Not you."

I stare at her, letting her words sink in. "I promised to catch you when you fell, and I wasn't there."

"Oh, Cameron." She cups her hands around my face. "You're here. You've done nothing but hold me up since the second this happened." She surprises me by tilting forward to press her lips against mine, the first time she's done that since before her attack. "If you want to help me, tell me everything you haven't told me. I need to know."

She's referring to everything that happened after the attack. All she knows is that he was arrested and he's in jail until his hearing, bail denied to him. I haven't told her all the details leading up to his arrest, and how she came to be rescued. Some of it's because I don't want her to have to relive what she already went through and also because I'm not proud of some of my actions. I purse my lips and nod once. "Okay, if that's what you really need, I'll tell you."

"I want to know everything." She demands.

"Let's get a glass of wine then." I reach into the cupboard to retrieve two glasses. "We're going to need them." I pour us each a glass, then we both move into the living room to sit down.

"From what we can gather, Bennett had been watching you since the night at the restaurant when you had dinner with him and the senator. Apparently bringing up Faith must have triggered a red flag to him. Then me dragging you out of there in handcuffs an even bigger flag that we were on to him possibly being the person who attacked Faith."

"How did he get Xander to text me when I got home that night?" I watch as she takes a drink of her wine, her brows scrunched together as her mind tries to piece the information together.

"He stole Xander's phone earlier that evening and used it to text you to trick you into coming over to the plaza as a trap." I clear my throat and shrug. "I guess the senator and Xander had begun spending a lot of time together at that point, only fueling the anger and resentment Bennett seemed to be fostering."

"Why was he so angry about that?"

I scoff, not realizing she hadn't pieced this part together yet. "Bennett was in love with the senator."

Her eyes pop wide. "What?" She shakes her head. "So why attack all of us? Why not just tell Martin?"

"Well, we know now, after the fact, and after talking to the senator, that Bennett did indeed profess his feelings, but the senator didn't feel the same. He said that Bennett seemed fine with his rejection, and assured him that working together would not be a problem." I scoff. "That obviously was a big, fat lie. And now, unfortunately, the senator is having to deal with the aftermath of having a personal staff member responsible for attacking women. He's not in an easy place."

"That makes me sad. Martin is actually a really good man and works tirelessly to better the lives of people in our city. Steven's actions will definitely have a ripple effect." She shakes her head, frowning. "I still don't understand why he started attacking women though, if he was in love with Martin?" She shifts on the couch, her hand pressing against her stomach, a small wince of pain apparent on her face.

"Are you okay?" I sit up, leaning toward her.

"I'm fine." She offers me a small smile. "The incision throbs sometimes out of the blue." She waves her hand as she settles against the back of the couch again. "Keep going."

"Well, Bennett is denying he beat anyone." I roll my eyes in disgust. "Even though we have DNA evidence linking him to four other women, and testimony from each of them stating they had participated in some kind of sexual encounter with the senator."

"Yes." She smirks, knowingly. "He likes to watch."

"Watch?" I ask, realizing too late that I probably shouldn't have.

"Women. Together. It got him off."

I stare at her, some of what she obviously must have participated in as an escort becoming clearer, my pulse picking up a notch. She sighs. "Don't Cameron." She scoots closer to me to place a hand on my knee. "Don't over analyze this. What came before you does not matter. At all."

"I know." She's right. I know she's right. Even though the

thought of it drives a small stake into my heart, I nod my head. "Anyway, we can only assume about why he was attacking the women associated with the senator since he denies it. But jealousy is a prominent factor. Removing the competition another. Especially since none of you were sexually assaulted."

"I guess that's something." She whispers, her fingers picking at the material of her pajama bottoms. I swipe her fingers into mine, entwining them, cinching them gently in silent agreement.

"So, you arrested him the next day?"

"The next night, yes." I look away, the next part harder for me to tell her. "I stayed at the hospital with you until you came out of surgery. Once Charlie and Trey assured me they would stay with you, I left and went to the main precinct to listen to the 9-1-1 call."

"Oh my god." She breathes out, her hand rising over her open mouth. "I forgot that I had called them." She looks at me, eyes wide. "But I was attacked before I could say anything."

"Everything was recorded." I have to look away from her at this point, the sound of her being dragged, of his fist hitting her, her voice begging him to stop, the last scream to fall from her lips followed by a loud thump as he called her a whore burned in my brain, a scar that would never heal, no matter how much time passed. I clear my throat and turn back to her. "You must have dropped your phone. We found it on the stairs, cracked, but still on."

"You heard everything." She surmises, her chest rising and falling quickly as her breathing increases, her scared eyes locking onto mine, her voice low when she speaks. "What did you do, Cameron?"

I lift the wine glass to my lips to drain what's left in the glass, then push to my feet. I set the glass on the table, then pace back and forth, my hands clenching and unclenching as I remember exactly what I did to him. I stop and finally face her. "The official statement is that he fell down a flight of stairs while trying to evade arrest."

"And the real story?"

"I beat him to a bloody pulp. I hit him until my fists started to bleed, and then I switched to my feet, kicking him repeatedly with my steel toe boots until the only thing coming out of his mouth was blood. If Brian hadn't pulled me off of him, I probably would have killed him." I look away again and let out a breath I didn't know I was holding, ashamed that the feeling I got from beating him was satisfaction instead of guilt. I had taken an oath to protect and to serve, and I let my personal feelings get in the way of keeping that oath.

She rises from the couch, setting her glass on the table next to mine as her feet move into my line of vision, stopping when she's next to me. Her fingers trail up my chest, then close around my face as she moves it so she can look at me. "Good."

"Good?" I counter, disbelief in my tone.

"Cameron, I wish you had killed him." She shakes her head. "So help me God, because I know it's awful to wish that on anyone, but he deserves it. What he did to me, what he did to Faith, and those other women." She collapses against me, her arms sliding around to hold onto me, her voice mumbling against my chest. "I wish he was dead."

I nod, my chin brushing against her hair, not saying a word, just understanding that him being dead would probably be the only way she would ever feel one hundred percent safe again in this world, and her having this wish was justified. I couldn't give that to her, but I could hold her in my arms, and I could do everything else in my power to make sure she felt safe otherwise.

CHAPTER
Twenty-Three

~Gabrielle~

It had been a month since I had been attacked, my bruises healed, my scars from the surgery and stitches, itchy, but finally no longer sore. I still hadn't returned to work, and at this point, I wasn't sure I wanted to. I felt safe in my apartment. Everything I needed was a phone call away, and everyone I knew here seemed safe to me. The hospital just had too many unknowns for me at this point.

Faith and I had grown closer over the last few weeks as she became a regular visitor here at my apartment, our shared trauma bonding us more than any sexual experience we had together ever could have. She had also left Temptations, and not for reasons so different than my own. When she told me her story, however, you could have knocked me over with a feather. She was definitely a girl with more than a few secrets; her relationship with Father Noah Thomas the most surprising of them all.

But it was Cameron who was my rock, my knight in shining armor, my constant beacon of light whenever I felt the darkness begin to pull me under. In the month since my attack, he'd stayed with me every single night but three. And those were spent with Willow. He was a man who when he decided to love, loved and protected fiercely. He was a man who had captured my heart and soul so completely that I no longer remembered what my life was like before he entered it. And even though I had come to realize this, I still hadn't shared these feelings with him. He still tip-toed around me like I was a butterfly with broken wings; too fragile to touch for fear of breaking me further.

I'd had enough and was ready for that to change. Ready for him to get off the damn sofa and hold me in his arms again. All night, every night, not just when a nightmare pulled me from my sleep. I was ready to feel like a woman again and needed him to know I wasn't a delicate china teacup that would shatter under his touch. I wanted to feel him against me again. Cameron was in court today for various cases, so I called Charlie, now so pregnant it was fair to say she only waddled, not walked, and told her we were having a spa day. At thirty-eight weeks pregnant, she was more than happy to accompany me for a day of pampering.

My driver pulled up to her address and stepped out of the vehicle to help her into the car. I couldn't help the laughter that spilled from me when her round bottom plopped heavily beside me in the back seat.

"Yeah, laugh it up, bitch." She groaned as she maneuvered her body into a comfortable position next to me. "Go ahead and make fun of your pregnant best friend."

"Oh, honey!" I reach over to hug her. "You're just the cutest damn knocked up chick ever. Really!"

"Yeah, yeah." She waves me off. "The sooner this little princess arrives, the better. I've had enough of the wonders and joys of pregnancy."

"I can only imagine." I scoot closer to her to lay my hand flat on her round belly. "Honestly though, what's it feel like when she's kicking around inside of you?"

She looks over at me, her eyes softening around the edges as the corners of her mouth lift in a small smile. "Magical." She sighs, placing her hand over the top of mine. "It's just you and this little person that you actually created inside of your body. After she's here, I'll have to share her with the world, but for now, it's just me and her."

"You look so beautiful right now Charlie." I bump my shoulder against hers. "Honestly. You're going to be the most amazing mom."

"And you're going to be the most amazing auntie." She drops her head on my shoulder. We ride like that, my hand on her belly, her daughter rolling around underneath it, until we arrive at the spa. The next three hours are spent getting our hair washed, blow dried, our bodies massaged, our legs waxed, and then our fingers and toenails done. It's the first day in a really long time I don't think about what happened to me. I just think about what's to come, with this new baby, with Cameron, and with my life.

I get home a little after three and stand in my closet for the next half hour trying to decide what to wear. I am absolutely going to seduce that man of mine when he walks through the door and need something that will wow him. I walk down the length of dresses, skimming my fingers across the fabrics as I go, stopping when I brush across blue satin. I reach up to pull the wrap dress off the rack, nodding my head to myself. The very dress I wore the first time he came to my apartment, and the first time we had sex. Yes, this is the perfect choice for starting over. I remove the robe I'm wearing and change into the dress, checking my reflection in the mirror when I'm done. I spin around, the bald spot on the back of my head barely noticeable under the extensions the hairdresser placed for me today. I feel good. Even if there are approximately ten thousand bees swarming around in my stomach right now.

I'm sitting on the couch when the door to the apartment opens, and he strides inside, his step faltering when his gaze lands on me. He's wearing a black suit, the standard, crisp white dress shirt he usually pairs with his suits underneath. And even though it's not the first time I've seen him in it, the desire that pools in my core would make you think it was.

"Hi, handsome." I rise off the couch, my feet bare as I saunter toward him.

"I know that dress." His steely gray eyes sweeping down my frame as I approach, the leather case he's holding casually tossed onto the table next to him.

I stop in front of him, placing my two hands flat against his chest, then push up on my tiptoes to capture his mouth against mine. "I've missed you."

His arm snakes around my waist pulling me flush to his body, his arousal already evident against my waist as I fuse against him. "I've missed you too." His other hand trails up the side of my neck to cup my face, the tiniest bit of pressure applied to tilt my head as he drops his mouth on mine. I slide my hands up around his neck, my fingers clutching onto him as he deepens our kiss, his tongue sweeping inside my mouth, his taste a pleasure I have denied myself for way too long.

I slide my fingers back down his neck, grasping onto the lapels of his jacket, pushing it off his shoulders onto the floor. Before the material even thumps to the floor, I begin working the buttons of his shirt, the desire to feel his bare skin under my hands causing my fingers to tremble.

"Here." His mouth breaks from mine, his hands gripping onto both sides of his shirt as he tugs hard, the buttons tearing from the shirt as it splits open to reveal his chiseled torso. My eyes pop wide as the little pieces of plastic bounce across the floor, and I lean forward, sealing my lips over one dark nipple, a moan vibrating from his chest, as his fingers tangle in my hair. I flick my tongue over the peak swelling in my mouth, then suck, his hips jolting against mine when I do.

"Oh babe." He groans above me when I release the suction on his nipple to lave my tongue over it. "That feels so good."

I tilt my head up to smile at him, gazing at him under my lashes. "I want to make you feel good."

His hand tilts my head up further to his as he gazes down at me. "Are you sure?"

I catch my lower lip between my teeth and nod against his hand. He bends, his arms moving behind my back and knees, then he stands tall, scooping me up, cradling my body to his as he carries me to the bedroom. When he reaches my bed, he lowers me onto its surface, his hands dragging out from under me, the fingers on one of his hands latching onto the tie at my side releasing the bow. His fingers splay wide across my stomach before one sweeps under the soft material of the dress to pull it open, my body naked underneath.

"Jesus, Gabby, you are so beautiful." His fingers graze softly over my flesh, my skin pebbling under his touch, my hand moving to cover the scar on the right side of my belly. He shakes his head, his hand covering mine to pull it gently away. "Don't." He bends over me, his lips pressing tenderly across the length of the scar, looking up at me. "You're beautiful, all of you, inside and out." My head falls back against the bed, my heart swelling, his lips grazing up the center of my stomach, stopping as he tugs my tight bud into his mouth.

I arch up into his heat, my eyes closing as every nerve in my body seems to center under his mouth, moisture pooling in my core as his fingers slide against my folds. I groan loudly, my legs spreading wide when he inserts a single digit, his palm grinding into my clit as I thrust my hips. I forgot how good this felt, and mutter this out loud as my fingers dig into his scalp.

He lifts off of me, my body instantly rising off the bed to retrieve his touch, but I still when I hear his belt releasing and see his pants slide off his waist, his hard length springing up against his belly. I reach for it, wrapping my fingers around its base as I guide it toward the juncture of my legs, crying out when he buries himself inside of me. His arms slide under my back lifting my chest up against his as he begins rocking his hips into mine.

I reach around his waist, one hand grabbing onto the back of his ass, my fingernails biting into his flesh I as try and force him to drive into me harder. Our lips find one another, our teeth clacking together each time he plunges against me, small gasps of pleasure panting from me when his hips begin to piston more quickly.

I claw onto him, desperate to feel him as close to my skin as possible, my body beginning to tingle as the walls surrounding his hard cock tighten, strangling his length as my entire body convulses then free falls, my pussy pulsing again and again around him. He thrusts into me a final time, his hot seed spurting inside of me as he bellows out my name.

He collapses on top of me, his weight a welcome assault against my body as my arms wrap around him, keeping him close to me, as I finally whisper the words I've been feeling since the first time I slept with him. "I love you, Cameron."

I feel his body stiffen under me, his arms moving to push himself off of me to look down at my face. His eyes lock onto mine, a smile lifting the corners of his mouth before he crushes it against mine. When he pulls back, he's still smiling. "I love you too, so much Gabby."

That night, Cameron sleeps in my bed again, with me, never feeling more safe or secure, in his arms. When we wake the next morning, he brings me coffee in bed, and we lay and talk for hours. We make two huge decisions, the first one easy, the second one terrifying, at least for me.

He's agreed to move in with me. He's been here every night for the past month anyway, and neither of us can imagine being without the other going forward. I'm still not sure what the future holds for me in terms of my job, but since money was never an issue for me anyway, I know I can figure that out as I go.

The second thing is meeting his daughter. He's told her

about me, so she knows he's seeing someone and understand that her dad has fallen in love. He assures me that Willow has only expressed excitement about meeting me and that I shouldn't be scared, but of course, I am. This is the most important woman in his life. I want her to like me, hopefully, love me one day. It's a Saturday, and a gorgeous April day, so after calling his ex-wife, we make arrangements to pick Willow up to take her to the park.

My heart is fluttering in my chest when we pull up outside of her building, and I watch as Cameron swings his darling little girl up into his arms, both of them smiling wide as they hug each other. The love between them is glaringly apparent, and slightly overwhelming when I think what I have to try to live up to. He carries her in my direction, and I decide to get out, wanting to meet her face to face instead of inside the car. He stops in front of me. "Willow, this is Gabby, the woman I told you about."

She cocks her head, her little braids flopping against one side of her face as she peers at me, a shy smile lifting her perfect pink lips. "Hi." She squeaks out.

"Hi." I say. "I'm really glad to finally meet you Willow."

Her hands reach out and her tiny fingers trail lightly around my eyes. "You have eyes like a mermaid tail."

I feel my cheeks lift into a wide smile. "You know, I've actually heard that before." I shift my gaze to Cameron, and it's in that instant this little girl completely and utterly consumes my heart, and that I know everything is going to be fine.

The End…..

I really hope you enjoyed Gabby's story. Tempting Teacher, the next story in the Tempting Nights Series will be releasing Summer 2024!

In the meantime, if you enjoyed Gabby's story, I would be so grateful if you could leave a review. It can be one sentence, but it makes such a difference in our books being seen.
Thank you so very much!
https://geni.us/temptingjustice

Also, if you liked the Tempting Series, take a look at my award winning series, The Auction Series. It's a billionaire, auction, dom-sub, secret identity love story that's full of twists that will keep you turning the pages.
The first book is called The Winning Bid and can be found here:
https://geni.us/winningbid

About the Author

Michelle Windsor is the author of over a dozen steamy, contemporary romances filled with alpha males and even stronger females. She has achieved both Amazon and Barnes & Noble International Best Seller status, and was awarded Best Contemporary Romance Writer by Passionate Plume Ink in 2019. Her first book, The Winning Bid, was nominated for the Summit Indie Book Awards by Metamorph Publishing in 2017, and continues to be her best-selling book to date.

Michelle is married with three grown children, and lives north of Boston in the type of suburban neighborhood you read about in sweet romance books, (not hers)! When she's not working on another book, you can find her spending time with her husband, hanging out with her three sisters, or snuggled up with her three cats, yes three, watching a movie or reading a book.

Keep up to date with Michelle on her web page:
https://www.authormichellewindsor.com

Also by Michelle Windsor

The Winning Bid:
https://geni.us/winningbid

The Final Bid:
https://geni.us/finalbid

The Ultimate Bid:
https://geni.us/ultimatebid

The Auction Series-Three Book Collection
https://geni.us/auctionseries

Losing Hope:
https://geni.us/losinghope

Love Notes:
https://geni.us/lovenotesbook

Catching Chase:
https://geni.us/catchingchase

Tempting Secrets:
https://geni.us/temptingsecrets

Tempting Tricks:

https://geni.us/temptingtricks

Tempting Justice:

https://geni.us/temptingjustice

Tempting Nights Box Set Collection, Books 1 - 3

https://geni.us/temptingnightsboxset

Taking Flight:

https://geni.us/takingflight

Just One Christmas:

https://geni.us/justonechristmas

Made in the USA
Columbia, SC
05 January 2025